D1520855

Dam Nation

E.J. Staffa

Author's Note

This is a work of fiction. While it is set against the backdrop of real historical events, including life in the 1920s and 1930s in Bayonne, New Jersey and Las Vegas, Nevada, and the construction of the Bayonne Bridge and Hoover Dam, many details have been altered, invented, or dramatized for the sake of storytelling. The characters are purely fictional.

I have taken creative liberties with certain aspects of the era, including elements of journalism, politics, and the managerial structure of the dam and the bridge's construction. While I have strived to capture the spirit of the time, I acknowledge, for instance, that the actual hiring processes for workers on the Bayonne Bridge and for dam workers was likely more sophisticated than what is portrayed here. Similarly, with regard to the dam. while corruption and exploitation certainly existed, I recognize that many dedicated, ethical individuals worked tirelessly to ensure worker safety and fair employment.

To those who may have had honest journalists or principled politicians in their family, or relatives in management who cared deeply for the men building the dam, I mean no offense. My intent was never to diminish the integrity of those who played a role in this extraordinary feat of engineering. Rather, I aimed to tell a compelling story that brings to life the grit, struggles, and triumphs of the era.

If any liberties taken with history misrepresent the legacy of those who contributed to this monumental achievement, I sincerely apologize. This story is, above all, a tribute to the workers who risked everything to build something greater than themselves --- a marvel that still stands today.

Acknowledgements

To my dad, who filled my head with stories when I was a child, all of which began with "Long ago and far away…"

And to my wife Judy, for a life that has helped me live at least some of it in my imagination.

And to my good friend Chat GPT, who answered countless questions like, "Did they have refrigerators in Las Vegas in 1930?" And, "How did cameras work in 1933?"

Chapter 1: The Floor

The smell woke him, then came the sound --- wet, violent, inhuman.

Miles sat up fast, the cold floor biting through his shirt. For a second, he wasn't sure if he'd dreamed it, but then came the choking. A low, gurgling rasp, like someone breathing through water --- sad --- and sadly familiar.

He scrambled to his feet and ran to the kitchen. Max was on the floor, face down in a slick puddle of vomit, convulsing. One bare leg twitched against the cabinets. His pants were soaked through at the back, a sour, spreading stain beneath him. The smell hit Miles in the throat --- sick, sharp --- full of danger.

"Max --- Jesus Christ --- Max!" He dropped to his knees and rolled him onto his side, head tilted up. Max's face was ghost-pale, lips tinged blue. Foam bubbled at the corners of his mouth, and he was barely breathing. His body was trying to take in air, but it had nowhere to go.

Miles shoved his fingers into Max's mouth --- past the yellow teeth, past the stench—and scooped out the thick clumps clogging his throat. His hands shook. He gagged once, bit it back.

Max jerked, spasmed, then gasped --- a ragged, sputtering breath that rattled through his chest. Miles held him there, on his side, until the spasms eased.

His fingers were coated in vomit. His shirt splattered, pants soaked through at the knees. The tile was cold and sticky beneath him. Max's body was slack now, half-awake but breathing.

For a long time, Miles didn't move. This wasn't the first time. Likely not the last. With a practiced memory, he got up and rinsed his hands under the sputtering tap, wiping them on the inside of his shirt. He found an old blanket and draped it over Max. Left the mess where it was.

In the bathroom, he showered, changed into his school clothes, and laced up his boots with quiet, methodical care. Outside, the wind howled down the alley between buildings. The radiator clanged to life in the other room. Miles stepped over the puddle, grabbed his bag, and walked out the door.

Chapter 2: Home in Bayonne 1928

Hat pulled tightly over his frigid ears, and bundled up like the rest of the students, Miles Tornero noticed nothing. Blocking out yet another harrowing morning at Max's, he sat absorbed in a tattered book reading about an ancient Himalayan civilization. He was one of the few students in the class who came to school to learn. Max may not have taught him how to dress or save money or drive a car, but he taught him there's a whole world beyond Bayonne, New Jersey. He couldn't read a whole book in an hour like Max nor read the paper in fifteen minutes and remember every word, but he loved the smell of the paper, the way the cover bent in his hands, and the mystery and surprise of whatever might be on the next page.

When a particularly powerful burst of wind pounded on the thin windows and demanded to be noticed, Miles broke out of his trance. Looking across rows of tenement houses and shops, he gazed emptily across the horizon at John D. Rockefeller's behemoth refinery on Constable Hook, "The Standard" as it was called, smelly, ugly, a confusing mess of massive oil tanks, billowing smokestacks, miles of curly pipes, and fumes. This was home.

At the ring of the dismissal bell, he marked his place, slapped the book closed, and trudged along in line out of class, making eye contact ever so briefly with Vanessa Holland, the most beautiful 16-year-old girl on Planet Earth. For a moment, he thought he saw a smile, but he couldn't hold the gaze. When he looked up, she was gone and he stepped out into the cold pale green corridor filled with noisy kids and rows of rusty metal lockers.

There was no home to go home to, not for two seemingly endless years. Instead, he'd head to Max's apartment and bring him the rest of his school lunch, thanks to the benevolence of one Dr. M.F. Corwin, who saw to it that undernourished students ate for free. Max would say of Corwin, "That's a real fuckin' saint alright I'll tell ya, not like them God damn miracle worker Italians those fuckers in Rome call saints."

Lately, Max was working nights at The Standard. Miles hated the thought of having to wake him up again, dress him, clean him, and make him go to work. When Miles walked in the door, Max was off the kitchen floor and now in his usual spot, sprawled naked on what used to be sofa, surrounded by cigarette butts. A neat stack of books marked, Property of Bayonne Public Library, lay next to him on the floor. A bottle of bootleg whiskey with an inch or two left at the bottom also lay on the floor, Max's enemy --- and friend --- from last night. As he often did, so as not to startle or embarrass him, Miles clattered loudly around the room to wake Max from his stupor.

"Hey Butchie Boy," Max said, surprisingly alert in an instant. Gray stubble covered his leathery face. Rail thin and maybe a few inches over five feet tall, he was only 45 years old --- but he looked well over sixty. He lit a cigarette and began his usual chatter, "I read about the Greek Gods today: Zeus, Hera, Aphrodite, Dionysus, you name 'em, I know 'em." Miles knew he did. As he arose from the sofa, his left leg bounced incessantly as it always did, driving intense energy into everything he said. Chesterfield dangling from his mouth, he added, "Did you know the whole damned Palace of Versailles didn't have one single bathroom? Fuckers just went and pissed and shit in the stairways. Damndest thing."

"Max, I want to hear all about it, but you need to get to work. Mrs. Murry came lookin' for your rent twice already this month." Max grumbled, "Fuck Mrs. Murry."

Miles didn't know if Max was sweeping floors or pumping pipes lately, didn't really matter, it changed all the time. Sammy Sweeny, his line manager, moved him around as much as possible to keep people from noticing. Had it not been for Sammy, Max would have lost his job years ago. But Sammy and Max were old friends. Sammy knew him when Max's wife and boy were still alive. He knew him before Max was even married.

Twenty-eight years ago, in the great Standard Oil fire of 1900, Max pulled Sammy out from under a burning horse cart and swatted out flames of angry oil dancing over his body. Sammy could never be sure Max even remembered the day that lighting struck an oil tank and set Bayonne ablaze for four days, driving massive floating fires across the waters of Upper New York Bay. Max never talked about it. Then again, Max never really talked about anything anymore, except to Miles.

A quick shower and a half sandwich later and they were out of Max's filthy apartment and on the streets of Bayonne. The 15-minute walk to the trolley stop would air Max out and stiffen him up a bit. Miles decided to go with him and make sure he got there.

The trolley line was dedicated to shuttling refinery workers off the polished city streets out Old Hook Road and into the center of Constable Hook. A few clangs of the trolley bell and a wave goodbye and Max was off to work, for at least one more day.

Miles mostly spent his after-school hours at the Bayonne Youth Center, or at his part time job at Charles Grotsky's Fine Men's Wear. Mr. Grotsky was good to Miles, although he could be harsh. He always compared Miles' work to Billy Flannagan's, gone now for over a year to join the army. Miles would always get the lecture on how important it was to serve one's country.

Though Grotsky couldn't really afford it, he let Miles work at the store a couple days a week, hanging and folding clothes, and unloading deliveries of the latest styles from around the world. Miles would look at all the fine garments and vow, "One day I'll wear a suit like that, I know it." But for now, he'd settle for the dollar or two he'd make a week; enough to buy a little food, soap, toothpaste, and maybe an article of clothing or two.

Today Miles would pay a nickel and hop the trolley line down Fifth Avenue to the Youth Center. On his way, he started getting spunky, jabbing a quick left hand, a sharp uppercut, and a finishing right cross against an imaginary opponent in front of him. Boxing was his salvation. At maybe five feet ten inches tall and 160 pounds, he needed more muscle --- but what he had packed a wallop. He beat almost anyone brave enough to step into the ring with him. He'd stand to toe to toe with anyone, even Joey Franco, who pummeled him the last time they put the gloves on.

The center was busy as usual. Sounds of bouncing leather basketballs and whirring jump ropes traveled on sweaty stale air. He turned quickly around a corner and bumped squarely into Pauley O'Donnell. "Watch where you're going WOP, or I'll flatten ya." Intimidated, Miles looked down and away and mumbled an apology. Slightly shorter and thinner than Miles, and almost a year younger, Pauley carried himself with an indefinable swagger that attracted respect and fear from his peers wherever he went. He seemed to own the youth center.

Angry with himself for backing down, Miles stepped into the ring with a kid he'd never met, ready to vent his frustrations. "Get ready to eat my leather," Miles said with his best tough-guy bravado. Now the big man he couldn't be minutes ago, Miles repeated some clever lines he'd heard before from older boys, "I don't know who you are or where you're from, but I'm about to teach you never to walk into another man's gym!" The stranger stared blankly forward, "bring it boy."

Miles sized up his opponent. He noticed only bright orange hair, pale hazel eyes, and more freckles on one body than he'd ever seen in his life. Before he could notice more, such as his opponent's massive chest and brick-sized fists, a ten-year-old water boy tapped a tiny silver bell. Miles charged out, unusually quickly and aggressively, ready for the kill. Moving frantically forward, he reared back his mighty left arm, aimed squarely at the middle of his foe's freckled face. But before he could release his blow, a lightning-fast jab landed flush on his nose blinding him with a flash of a million exploding silvery stars. In ten seconds, Miles awoke, flat on his back. Too embarrassed to still feel angry, he thought to himself, 'Stupid! Didn't Max tell you, never fight in anger?'

Chapter 3: Leaving Home 1924

Two days into their 1,256-mile car ride from Lincoln, Nebraska to Las Vegas, Nevada, the McGuire family sat in near silence. The journey seemed endless, and the relentless heat of the summer sun bore down on them. The gravel roads rattled beneath their wheels as their 1912 Ford Model T groaned along, the old engine coughing with every mile.

Nancy's mood was as hot and oppressive as the weather. Her back was pressed against the vinyl seat, sticky with sweat, but she hardly noticed the discomfort. Her eyes, narrow and angry, avoided her husband, Robert, who was gripping the wheel with a determined, stone-faced expression. The silence between them was almost suffocating. Nancy's anger had simmered for days, months even. But today it was on the verge of boiling over. She refused to look at him, refused to acknowledge his presence in any way. Her gaze was fixed firmly out the passenger window, her eyes locked on the endless, dusty flatlands, the world outside a blur of brown and heat.

Robert's face was etched with lines of weariness and determination. He had long since given up trying to make conversation. He tried, once, maybe twice, to speak, to reassure Nancy that this was a good thing --- that moving to Las Vegas, and eventually to the Boulder Dam project, would change their lives. But she didn't want to hear it. She had heard too many promises before. She did not want to hear again, "a fresh start," or, "a new chance," and yet, here they were --- on the edge of nowhere, their future uncertain.

Her silence gnawed at Robert. He was never good with silence. In the early days of their marriage, silence had been easy. But now, after their recent struggles, it felt like the weight of the world pressing down on him, suffocating him.

The decision to leave was his, but Robert believed it was the only option. The farming life they worked so hard to build back in Nebraska had crumbled under the weight of drought and economic despair. They had lost everything: the crops, the land, the sense of security they had once taken for granted. The Great War was over, but the financial repercussions were still being felt. As the country struggled to find its footing in the early 1920s, Robert had heard talk of new opportunities in the West. He heard about the Boulder Canyon Project --- the start of building the world's largest dam --- a project that was still in its infancy but was already being touted as something that could bring jobs and prosperity to the area.

In his mind, it sounded like the perfect solution. A new start, away from the ghosts of Nebraska. A chance to rebuild, to provide for his family once again. He found the promise of work in the dam project and saw it as a lifeline --- maybe even salvation. So, when word of the opportunity reached him, he had taken it, despite his wife's objections. He didn't expect her to be happy about it --- after all, it meant leaving the only home she had ever known --- but he pressed forward. Robert wasn't sure what the future would hold, but he knew that staying in Nebraska wasn't an option.

And now, they were headed West on dirt roads to a place none of them had ever seen, to a life none of them could imagine. Robert's mind raced with visions of the dam, the construction, the bustling workforce that would pour into the Nevada desert, transforming it into something new. He could almost see it in his mind: men working with steel, building something massive, something monumental. He thought that, surely, this would be the opportunity to turn things around. A job. A place to live. A fresh start.

But as the miles stretched on, the weight of uncertainty began to press down on him. What if this wasn't the answer? What if the dam project didn't succeed? What if, after all the miles, all the sacrifices, there was nothing waiting for them but disappointment and regret?

In the back seat, 12-year-old Becky sat nervously, sensing the tension that hung in the air. Normally, she would have complained about the heat, the boredom, the monotony of the trip. But today was different. Today, she sensed that the silence wasn't just about the long car ride --- it was about something else. Something more serious. Something that had been building between her parents for a long time.

She had seen the way her mother's eyes narrowed whenever her father spoke. Heard the sharpness in Nancy's voice when she responded, or rather, when she didn't. She could feel the distance between them. It wasn't just the car ride or the dust or the heat. There was something deeper --- a rift that had opened between her parents, one that Becky didn't know how to fix. It was as though the love that had once filled their home had faded, replaced by something harder, deeper.

But Becky didn't dare to speak. She knew better. She wasn't sure if talking would make things better or worse, but either way, she didn't have the words for what was happening. Instead, she stared out the window, her face pressed against the hot glass, watching the flat plains stretch on and on.

Her thoughts drifted to the future, to the strange and mysterious promise of Las Vegas. What would it be like there? The name itself seemed foreign, like a place from a storybook. She had heard stories about the West --- stories of wild adventures, of cowboys and outlaws, of cities that grew up out of the desert. She had heard whispers of men who came to the land and made fortunes, and others who came and lost everything. It seemed like a place where anything could happen, and maybe, just maybe, this was their chance to change their lives.

Finally realizing why her anger was particularly strong today, Nancy broke the silence. "I can't believe we're doing this because your brother told you about it. You know I adore Albert, but he hasn't been successful at anything, but you trust him to do this? You don't have the faintest idea what he's doing out there, but we're following right behind him." She crossed her arms, "Great move," she said sarcastically.

Becky's ears perked up and her heart dropped. She had no idea this move had anything to do with Albert. She suppressed a gasp, sunk deeper into her seat, and with fear shaking her entire body, thought to herself, "Please God no --- not Uncle Albert!"

Chapter 4: Poison

Sore, tired, and deflated from his beating at the gym, Miles retreated to the library, to spend the rest of his evening in peaceful solitude.

As he limped to his usual seat, Mrs. Macintyre, the head librarian, looked sternly over the rims of her thick black glasses. Her look seemed to say, as usual, "And will we be being quiet today Mr. Tornero?" He'd never know, but Mrs. Macintyre cried most every time she saw him.

She looked at him like that to try to convey some motherly wisdom, because she had nothing else to offer. She knew Miles was an orphan with no legal guardian. She didn't know how the School Board still believed he lived on the north end of Broadway with his Uncle Henry, given his uncle hadn't stepped foot in town in over two years, but she never said anything. She knew they'd take the boy and put him in an orphanage, a fate she thought much worse than living and surviving on the streets. She knew it did no good, but she kept Henry Tornero's library card in active status, to somehow help protect the struggling teen.

Settled, Miles decided to read again about his favorite historical icon, Napoleon Bonaparte. He enjoyed reading how Napoleon would conquer much larger armies by separating their forces, then defeating each smaller unit. But Miles was equally amazed how someone as brilliant as Napoleon could have blundered so badly in the winter of 1812, being lured into the depths of the Russian winter only to get so far before realizing that a retreating enemy had scorched all the land, forcing him to retreat, an army of 450,000 diminished to 10,000. As Miles gently moved his nose from side to side, thankful it wasn't broken, he had to laugh to himself, 'At least I didn't fuck up as bad as Napoleon today.'

Tonight, would be bitterly cold; too cold to sleep under the railroad trestles. He looked forward to spring, when he could once again spend his nights gazing up at the stars from under the tracks. Instead, as he'd been doing lately, he'd spend the night at Max's.

Max never seemed to care whether Miles came or went, but somehow, he treated him as if he were always there. If he didn't see Miles for two days, Max might pick up on the very next sentence where he left off the last time he was jabbering to Miles; left leg bouncing, bouncing, bouncing, so powerfully it could shake the whole room. It simply never stopped. Miles loved Max. He was the only adult in the world who didn't judge him.

When he came into Max's apartment after the library closed, he noticed Max was hunched over a tiny desk in his bedroom reading a book about poisons. Miles was upset to see Max left work early again. He yelled in a hello but Max snapped, "Not now I'm busy." Staying out of Max's way, Miles sat on a rickety wooden chair and continued reading about Napoleon.

After an hour or so, Max emerged, himself again. "Hey there Butchie boy, see this?" Max held a tiny foil packet. "Rat poison, Got it right at the grocery --- Lyon's Poison Cheese, 93.5% pure arsenic. Ground it up real fine in my daddy's mortar and pestle." Give a guy a plug o' this stuff the size of a nickel and he's a goner in half an hour."

Pointing to a tiny drawer in a piece of furniture sitting randomly against a bare wall, Max said, "Gonna keep it right there in case Mrs. Murry comes around again lookin' for rent money." Miles was not amused. "Max, you know you're not going to do that," he said. Max answered, "Never know Butchie boy, never know."

Miles knew Max would never poison anyone. "Just keep it away from me, please, I got enough problems." Max shrugged and answered, "Yeah you do. Looks like you got the shit beat outta you today." Miles, in no mood to talk about it, answered, "How'd you guess?" Max didn't answer, he just wandered back to his room and went to bed.

Bed seemed like a good idea for Miles too. Not daring to go near Max's soiled sofa, he grabbed a balled-up blanket and lowered himself onto the hard wooden floor. He pulled out a handkerchief from his shirt pocket and placed it over his nose and mouth, a futile attempt to block the incessant smells of stale urine and vomit that never left Max's flat.

Sleep escaped him, so Miles lay awake and tried to make sense of Max's fascination with poison and realized this was only one of a million things he didn't know about his friend. Although he felt he knew Max, he realized he really knew nothing about Max. Max told him facts about the world, myriad pieces of endless information from a brain that never forgot a thing. Indeed, on the day they were handing out photographic memories and brains, Max Hirschfield got more than his fair share of both.

Miles never knew where Max came from, or what brought this genius of a man to be working as a line worker in a Bayonne refinery. Miles never knew that Max flew through high school and finish college in only two years. He didn't know that Max married a beautiful young student and became the youngest professor ever to teach at Rutgers University, or that by the beginning of 1918, Max and his wife had a strapping two-year old son and that Max had already conducted award winning research in pharmacology, politics, and physics.

But what Miles also didn't know was that all of that idyllic life ended abruptly for Max, like it did for so many others in that year. One October afternoon, when Max arrived home from class, his normally hearty child lay listless in his bed. Mother by his side, a doctor with a white linen cloth tied over his mouth tended to the child. Gravely, the doctor shared the news with the confused parents. The Spanish flu pandemic of 1918 had come to northern New Jersey.

The child passed in two weeks' time, followed by his mother only days after. The day his son died was the last day Max ever spent on the college campus.

Eventually Sammy got him his job back on the line at Standard Oil Works, where Max remained, memories frozen in time for the last ten years. Miles knew nothing of that past, nothing of a man's shattered life. He knew only of a friend who didn't seem to fit in the world around him.

Chapter 5: Betrayal

The desert stretched endlessly before Albert, an unforgiving expanse of dust and heat, where men like him could disappear, live outside the law, and do what needed to be done. He thought from time to time how his life in Lincoln, Nebraska had turned to --- this. His hideout was nothing more than a cabin built into the side of a rocky hill, hidden by scrub brush and surrounded by land so empty it swallowed men whole. It was the perfect place for a man with a past like his.

Albert was a brute of a man, tall and powerful, his thick arms hardened by years of labor and violence. His left hand, however, was a twisted ruin --- his fingers curled unnaturally, curled, stiff, and useless. It had been that way since birth, a deformity that had shaped his entire life. He remembered the taunts, the whispers, the girls in school recoiling at the sight of it. He remembered the rage that built inside him every time he caught someone staring, the way his mother told him to ignore it, and the way his father told him to toughen up.

But the worst of it --- the one memory that never left --- was Nancy. Nancy, who never mocked him. Nancy, who treated him kindly when no one else did. Nancy, who he could only love from afar. Nancy, who had chosen Robert instead. Albert hated Robert for it, but more than that, he hated the kind of man Robert was --- honest, hardworking, respected. Albert had none of those qualities. He had left Lincoln, Nebraska, telling Robert he was heading West to be a fur trapper, a man of adventure. That had been a lie. He had no interest in trapping. He was drawn to the one business that truly thrived in the shadows --- bootlegging.

Now, years later, Albert sat at a crude wooden table in his cabin, staring at a letter he had yet to finish. It was addressed to Robert. He had written half a page, but the words mocked him. He wanted to sound casual, like a long-lost brother catching up, but his real intent was far from innocent. He was broken and desperate. His last bootlegging deal had gone to hell, and if he didn't find a way out soon, he'd be a dead man.

It was supposed to be an easy job. He and his partner, Clyde Reilly, had arranged to smuggle a shipment of whiskey down from Utah, through the desert, and into Nevada. There was always a demand for liquor in Las Vegas, and Albert had a reputation as a man who could get things done. But Albert was never one for sharing. The money was too good, and Clyde was a fool. Albert had it all planned --- the moment Clyde got comfortable, the moment he let his guard down, Albert struck. They had camped out in a ravine, the crates of liquor stacked in the truck. The fire crackled, and Clyde had been talking, rambling about his plans, about how he wanted to move up in the world.

Albert listened, nodded, and when the moment was right, he shot Clyde in the chest and rolled him into a shallow grave he had dug earlier. Easy. But fate was cruel. As Albert drove the truck toward their buyers, headlights appeared. Another crew --- rival bootleggers, men who had been watching. Before Albert could react, gunfire tore through the windshield, forcing him to abandon the truck and run. By the time he made it back to his hideout, the shipment was gone. The money was gone. Clyde was dead, and now

Albert had nothing but a letter to Robert. He felt no remorse. The world owed him for his misfortune. Taking Clyde's part of the profits would have been just a small piece of that debt.

Albert forced himself to finish the letter. He lied and wrote that fur trapping up in Nevada's Ruby Mountains was lucrative for a while but it's been declining and he's planning a move south, closer to Las Vegas --- a great time to visit and catch up on old times. But he really needed money --- and --- to see Nancy. The memory of her was still fresh, still powerful. She had been kind to him, but she chose Robert. She'd built a life with him. Albert spent years trying to forget her, but he never could. And then there was Becky, the girl he saw as just like all the others who rejected and mocked him. She wasn't a small child anymore. Albert licked his lips.

Yes, it was soon time for a visit. He folded the letter and sealed it. He had no money, no liquor, and no allies left. But he had family. And family always helped. They would help him. Or they would regret it.

Chapter 6: Survival

His youthful body now recovered from yesterday's pounding at the gym, Miles woke the next morning in Max's apartment. He flipped a light switch scattering dozens of cockroaches scurrying to safety. Today was Saturday, a day to rest and relax.

Miles looked for Max and saw him standing outside in his undershorts on the rusty fire escape. "Come on in, Max, it's freezing out there!" Miles would have gone out to get him, but he couldn't stand the thought of looking down. One of Miles's few memories of childhood was falling out of a tree he once defeated by climbing to the very top. A few well-placed branches prevented serious injury, but ever since, he was deathly afraid of heights. Max came inside with no explanation. "Good morning Butchie."

"Butchie I'm goin' down to the river this morning," said Max. "Read in the paper there's gonna be eight big barges come in today bringin' loads of rocks to start the bridge. This is gonna be some bridge,

Butchie boy, the biggest goddamn steel arch bridge in the world. Right here in Bayonne." Looking forward to seeing progress on the building of the Bayonne Bridge, Miles said, "I'll go too, looks like a nice day."

The barges struggled mightily against the choppy currents of the Kill Van Kull, loaded with heavy boulders that would shore up the road ramps on either side that would eventually produce a bridge and allow passage from the southern tip of Bayonne to Staten Island. One by one, they off loaded their cargo into the river, huge waves splashing all around as the boulders disappeared beneath the surface.

Max stared thoughtfully across the water, "Man don't seem to stand up too well against nature, Butchie, but sometimes all it takes is time. Mother Nature always wins when she wants to win, but if man is strong enough, if he tries his best, she can be a good mother. Sometimes, given time, she lets man feel like he can make a difference." Miles listened silently to Max simply being Max.

As the last empty barge turned north and into Upper New York Bay home towards Manhattan, a medium sized dog with bright white fur and light brown patches walked up to Max and placed both paws on his thighs. Max reached down and patted the dog's head. "Hey Nicky-boy," he said admiringly. "Did you tear any other dog's throat out today, run any out on a rail?" Max looked over at Miles. "Ya know I'm the only human this dog will let touch him, he don't trust nobody." Nicky stepped down. Max and Miles watched the dog trot off the beach and up onto First Street, next to a nearby dumpster at the back of a short alley.

Miles could tell Max was still feeling philosophical. "That's king fuckin' dog of the streets right there Butchie, don't look like it does it?" Miles shook his head to agree. "He ain't the smartest or the biggest or the fastest, but put 'em all together and he is king dog. I watch him and think, ya gotta be smart and big and fast, but ya don't gotta be the smartest, or the biggest, or the fastest, ya just gotta be smart enough, and big enough, and fast enough, to matter, get it?"

As Max finished his lecture, a big black German Shepherd slinked from around the other side of the dumpster --- face-to-face with Nicky. "I ain't never seen that dog around here," said Max. Both dogs stood motionless. The shepherd jumped first. His heavy paws thundered down on Nicky's back and buckled his knees. Cornered and stunned, Nicky saw a small opening between the wall and the dumpster. Without hesitation, he blasted through, sprinting far out of sight. The shepherd circled around and howled in proud victory.

Miles looked at Max, confused. Raising his index finger to his temple, Max observed, "See that Butchie, smart dog, knows it's about survivin' on the streets, not winnin,' see? He knew he had the bad ground, had no way to win. He'll wait till the fight is on his terms. But I'll tell ya one thing Butchie. As sure as I know my own name, that big black dog will be dead in no time." Taking a long puff on his cigarette, he stared at the German Shepherd and muttered, "I guaranfuckin' tee it."

Chapter 7: A New Home in Las Vegas, 1928

Las Vegas was no longer just a dusty railroad stop. With the promise of a massive dam project looming on the horizon, it was slowly building with new arrivals—workers, businessmen, gamblers, and drifters, all carving out their place in the desert. Among them were the McGuire's, who, after their harrowing journey West, had finally begun to build a stable life.

Robert had steady work on the Clark County road construction crew, laboring under the scorching Nevada sun. The work was grueling and dangerous, but it paid well enough, and Robert took pride in knowing he was helping build the arteries that would one day lead to something even greater --- the Boulder Dam. He came home each evening covered in dust, his muscles aching but his spirit high, carrying stories of near accidents, cracked equipment, and the reckless men who worked alongside him. His stories never quite jived with those in the newspapers saying what a tight ship the road department ran.

Nancy, ever resourceful, made their sparse living quarters into a home. Their small rented house was just a dot on the edge of town, but she filled it with warmth, stitching curtains for the windows and setting a small garden in the back despite the relentless desert heat. She stretched every dollar and bartered at the market. She even earned some extra money by helping out at The Desert Sun, editing letters to the editor. She was a wiz with words as a student and realized that in some small way, she was helping independent news fight against corrupt big-city newspapers that controlled the town's information. She would learn later of the depths of that corruption.

Becky, now a teenager, thrived in her new surroundings, though she remained wary of the rougher elements of Las Vegas life. She attended school, but more than that, she became an integral part of the local church, which became a center of community life. Through the church, Nancy and Becky met many of the honest, hardworking families in town, and it gave Becky a sense of purpose --- helping with Sunday school, organizing charity efforts, and learning about the struggles of families like her own.

One late afternoon, Nancy and Becky set out on a shopping excursion into town. The streets were lively and growing, filled with workers looking for a drink after a long day, gamblers seeking their fortunes, and merchants hawking everything from fresh produce to secondhand furniture. Their first stop was the market, where Nancy carefully selected flour, beans, and fresh vegetables, calculating the cost in her head as Becky helped carry the bags.

As they finished their shopping, Nancy glanced up toward the post office and hesitated. "Becky, why don't you check if there's any mail at the post office?" Becky nodded and headed that way, but Nancy hesitated again and quickly changed her mind. "Actually, never mind," she said. "You finish up the other errands. I'll check myself."

Becky shrugged, not thinking much of it, and turned toward the general store. Nancy made her way to the post office, the air cooling slightly as the sun dipped lower in the sky. Inside, the clerk recognized her and handed her a letter --- the handwriting familiar --- simply addressed to Robert McGuire, Las Vegas. Nancy's breath caught. Could it be from Albert? They hadn't heard from him in so long. She thought to herself what a nice surprise, Robert and Becky would be so pleased! But she wouldn't open it, she'd wait and give it to Robert and let him get the wonderful news. When she reached her daughter, Becky immediately sensed something was up. "Everything okay, Mama?" Nancy smiled broadly. "Yes, sweetheart, more than ok. It looks like we have a letter from Uncle Albert. I'll bet he wants to visit. Let's get home and share the good news with Dad!"

Betraying the terror that sprung up inside, Becky somehow managed a smile, continuing to hide the secret she has held so long. She seethed realizing how close she came to being able to intercept that letter, then wondered if it would really have made a difference. Again, she whispered to herself, "Please God no --- not Uncle Albert!" But one way or another, it seemed Albert was coming back into her life. Her fear seemed to magnify the heat of the intense Nevada sun, and she felt herself melting away.

Chapter 8: Blue

Winter in Bayonne wore on, day after same cold day. While most days were the same as the next, Miles would start each one convincing himself this one would be different. Usually in the morning, if he spent the night at Max's, he'd look in the only mirror in Max's apartment, comb his hair and say, "Today is the day I talk to her." He'd bolster his courage, imagine success, but in the end, whenever he came face-to-face with Vanessa Holland, no words came out. He'd try but he couldn't, terrified that whatever came out of his mouth would be the stupidest most inappropriate thing she'd ever heard.

Christmas came and went like any other boring day. Miles tried to get Max to do something, maybe even go to New York City and see the lights and action he'd only heard about from others. But Max would not be moved. In fact, if it were possible, Max was drunker Christmas morning than Miles had ever before seen him. New Years Eve was not much different.

But Max was not well. Little by little Miles noticed his decline. It was hard to tell the differences between the ravages of a brutal hangover and some other illness. When Max was hungover, which was almost all the time, he was like a bag of rags; dirty, foul, motionless, useless. But with each passing day, Miles noticed a strange effort to Max's breathing, especially after he climbed the stairs to his apartment. He couldn't put together more than a few words without coughing, constantly coughing. And most peculiar to Miles, he noticed that Max seemed to be turning blue. Miles didn't have a word for it. He just knew his friend was sick and getting sicker. If either of them could have paid a doctor, Miles would have known to call it emphysema.

As spring turned to summer, Miles found himself staying at Max's almost every night. Max needed help, and, both fortunately and unfortunately, being unemployed, Miles had a lot more time on his hands lately. Right after the Fourth of July, Miles walked into his job at the clothing store for his usual Tuesday afternoon shift and found a serious and somber greeter at the door. Mr. Grotsky got right to the point, "Miles, I can't let ya' work here no more." Stunned Miles looked at his boss but said nothing. "Listen boy, I like you, but Billy Flannagan's brother needs a job. His wife's gonna have a baby and I gotta help out Billy, gotta take care of our boys in uniform." Just like that, Miles added unemployment to his list of challenges in life.

Chapter 9: Darkness

Las Vegas in the late 1920s was a town of dual identities. By day, it was a bustling hub of promise, a growing city where workers built roads and houses and infrastructure in anticipation of something greater. By night, it transformed --- a place where deals were made in the shadows, where money exchanged hands in smoky backrooms, and where the powerful shaped reality to fit their needs.

Nancy had known life would be difficult here. She had braced herself for hardship, for the struggle of raising Becky and making ends meet. But what she had not anticipated was the creeping sense that something was deeply, irreparably, wrong beneath the surface of this town.

She first noticed it in whispers --- small things that nagged at her. A fellow church member mentioned how her husband lost his job at the railroad despite the papers claiming it was thriving. Another woman spoke about a land dispute where a family was forced off their property, only for it to be sold to a wealthy developer days later. These stories disturbed Nancy, but she could never be certain they were all true.

Then there were the newspapers. Nancy had always been an avid reader, taking an interest in the affairs of the town. But as time passed, she began to see patterns. A restaurant that had served her the worst meal of her life was raved about in the local paper --- "Best steak in Las Vegas!" the article proclaimed. A friend had been overcharged at a general store, only for the same store to be glorified in an editorial about its "honest business practices." It was all too perfect, too polished. And yet, these small deceptions seemed harmless compared to what she would soon uncover.

One afternoon, while out running errands, Nancy stepped into a small shop to buy fabric for new curtains. The clerk stepped to the back to retrieve what she needed. As Nancy waited, she would soon find out the store served another purpose. Nancy overheard voices in the next room --- two men speaking in hushed but heated tones. "Doesn't matter if the railroad's struggling," one voice said. "We print what we're paid to print." Nancy's brow furrowed. The second man scoffed. "You think people want the truth? No, they want to hear the railroad's booming, that the town's thriving, that we're on the verge of greatness."

Nancy held her breath. The voices belonged to a local journalist and a businessman, their conversation revealing exactly what she had begun to suspect --- the news was being manipulated. One of them chuckled. "People don't want reality. They want the story we sell them." Nancy stood frozen, the weight of realization pressing down on her. If the newspaper was willing to fabricate success stories about the railroad, what else had they lied about? What other truths had been buried beneath a smokescreen of deceit?

She left the store in a daze, the fabric purchase forgotten. As she walked down the dusty streets, past the saloons and people going about their daily lives unaware of what went on behind the scenes, she saw the town differently. This was not just a place of opportunity --- it was a place where power dictated reality.

She thought of Robert, out there working on the roads, trusting in the system, believing he was part of something great. She thought of Becky, growing up in a world where lies were dressed as truth. A chill ran through her. Las Vegas was not just a harsh and primitive town on the rise. It was a dangerous place, and if she wasn't careful, it would eat her alive.

Chapter 10: Optimism

On a brutally hot August Saturday morning in Bayonne, Miles awoke again in his usual spot on Max's floor. He wasn't happy about being unemployed, but he felt good today: a little sore but good. Yesterday he got his long-awaited revenge against Joey Franco in the boxing ring. Instead of standing with him toe-to-toe, Miles danced around Joey, popping him with jabs, aggravating him until he got impatient. At just the right time, when Joey got sloppy, Miles unloaded a haymaker that sent Joey into next week. Sweet revenge.

Still sleepy, he looked across the room and saw his gray flannel pea coat, his woolen hat, and his winter boots sitting in a dormant pile. Just months ago, he couldn't even go outside without those garments. But today, only ten o'clock in the morning, the heat had already conquered the tiny apartment. Rubbing sleep from his eyes, he wandered into the kitchen, found coffee and started reading an already-read newspaper. Max was up early.

Bright and alert this morning, Max wandered in and sat, "Morning Butchie boy." Then, seemingly out of nowhere, left leg bouncing so hard it rattled a crooked picture on the wall behind him, Max said, "Go down to the Bayonne Bridge work site on Tuesday morning, ask for Carl Callahan. Tell him Sammy Sweeney sent ya." After Miles lost his job at Grotsky's, Max hounded Sammy, day after day, to call in a chit with a friend out on the bridge to get Miles a job. He knew he was pushing his luck. He knew Sammy was already going out of his way for Max. But Max didn't care. He'd do anything for Miles.

Miles was confused, "You got me a job?" Max answered, "Sammy said they need help there, so I told him you were lookin', ya got lucky kid. I didn't do nuthin' just passed your name along, see?" With a giant smile Miles reached out and hugged his friend. Averse to touch, Max shrank his tiny body as Miles engulfed him into his broad chest. Oblivious to his friend's rancid odor, he hugged hard and beamed "I'm going to build the biggest God damn fuckin' steel arch bridge in the fuckin' world!"

Concealing a smile prompted by his young friend's feigned comfort with profanity, Max switched topics, "Readin' the paper? Atta boy. Lots in there today." In his new raspy, emphysema-soaked voice, Max continued after a vicious bout of coughing, "I just finished readin' it." Miles knew it likely had taken Max all of fifteen minutes to read the entire thing. He also knew he had it memorized, not just in general, but word for word. Likely to be employed and happy after months of drudgery, Miles was in the mood for a little fun. Sitting up straight and jutting out his chest in mock intimidation, Miles began to quiz Max on the entire contents of the August 31st, 1929 edition of The Bayonne Times.

Miles started with a random spot somewhere in the middle of the section of newspaper he was holding in his hands, and challenged Max, "What's on page A4?" Max took a wheezy breath and began with the most prominent headline on that page, "Two Negroes Lynched by Mississippi Mob," he said. With another labored breath he began rattling off the entire article, "Brook Haven, Mississippi: A crowd of angry white townspeople stormed the city's jail yesterday and apprehended two young negro males accused of assaulting two white men in an altercation reportedly related to a traffic incident. After charging past a lightly protected front desk, the crowd removed the captives and lynched them in a nearby park. According to witnesses..." Okay, enough of that one," said Miles.

He found another section of the paper, "What's on the sports page?" In a second Max switched gears and announced, "Yankees Blank Athletics, 2 to 0: Still Behind by 12-Games." Without stopping, "For a brief moment yesterday, the Yanks looked like champions again, even though their 2-to-0 victory over the Athletics did no more than reduce the thirteen-game first-place lead of the Mackmen to a comfortable 12. Ace Yankee pitcher Tom Pipgras held Connie Mack's squad hitless until the eighth inning. However, of special concern to Yankees fans, Babe Ruth struck out three times and left the game due to a lame back. Ailing manager Miller Huggins has not been able to..." Miles interrupted, "Okay, Max, I think you got that one nailed too."

"Last one," said Miles, what's on page A2? "This one's much more interesting," said Max. He again started with the headline. "Boulder Dam Design Selected: U.S. to Open Construction Bidding if Wilbur Can Generate Revenue Model." Max interjected some commentary before beginning, "Now here's a fuckin' thing worth memorizing. The government's gonna build the biggest God damn dam in the fuckin' world. It's gonna be so fuckin' big you can use all the concrete from every other dam ever built so far in this country to try to build it and you still wouldn't have enough concrete to build this fucker."

As quickly as he diverted, he got back on track, "After reviewing designs of 30 final proposals, Chief Engineer of the U.S. Reclamation Service, Raymond Walter today announced that the U.S. government has selected a final design for the Boulder dam, envisioned to tame the mighty Colorado river and bring irrigation and electricity to millions of people residing in seven states surrounding the river's tidal basin. The design calls for a massive concrete monolith 726.4 feet high, 660 feet thick at the base, and 1,282 feet long. President Herbert Hoover has been quick to warn that no plans will move forward until a funding mechanism has been found for the project, a job that will fall to Interior Secretary, Ray Lyman Wilbur. On December 21, 1928, President Calvin Coolidge signed into law authorization of the $165 million Boulder Canyon Dam Project Act...." Got it Max," said Miles interrupting again. "Hold on there, Butchie Boy," this one's worth talkin' about."

Miles sat back on a small wooden chair, preparing for a typical education session as only Max could issue. Max continued, "This thing's gonna be 60 stories high, taller than the fuckin' Woolworth Building. But it's gonna take years before you even see somethin' that even looks like a dam. First, they gotta make a dry spot where they build the dam, gonna dig four giant tunnels and make the whole fuckin' river go through 'em and around the spot where they build. And this ain't no regular river. This is the wildest God damn river on earth. Yes sir, Butchie Boy, they got this one figgered. It'll be easy as pie to get that funding. Ain't gonna cost Uncle Sam a penny in the long run. Before one fuckin grunt touches a shovel, they'll sell the rights to all the millions of kilowatts of energy this thing's gonna make. This big fuckin' hunk o' concrete's gonna light up the fuckin' desert and make farms outta sand."

Miles didn't understand it all. But it took a lot to impress Max. If Max was all aglow about it, it must be big and important. He liked when Max got excited about something. It seemed to happen less and less these days.

As Miles was about to fold up the newspaper and set it aside, he noticed a prominent advertisement directly next to the dam article. Amidst pictures of flying airplanes, the advertisement shouted, "See the Greatest Air Show on Earth! Come One Come All! Games! Prizes! The Greatest Flying Machines Ever Built! See Charles Lindbergh's Favorite Plane, the Velie Monocoupe 70! The ad said the show would start Labor Day, at noon, Monday, September 2, 1929, on the grounds of the exclusive La Tourette Hotel, located on the southern tip of Bayonne at the lower end of Broadway in an area of the city known as Bergen Point. Miles was fascinated, intrigued, he was determined to use some of his hard-earned money and see this show --- see a part of the world he'd never know.

Chapter 11: The Visitor

The knock at the door came as Nancy was preparing dinner. It was sharp, deliberate --- three raps, then silence. Robert glanced up, brow furrowing. He hadn't been expecting anyone.

"I'll get it," he said, pushing up from an old sofa. Becky felt her stomach knot. She had known, ever since overhearing her father mention Albert's letter, that he was somewhere in Nevada. But she had clung to the hope that he would stay far away, just passing through on his way to some miserable camp in the hills. Now, as her father pulled open the door, that hope shattered.

Albert stood in the doorway, a hulking figure against the fading light of dusk. He filled the frame --- broad-shouldered, thick-limbed, his presence somehow larger than it should have been. His face was rough, weathered by years of hard living, but his expression was a mask of warmth, the kind that could fool most people.

"Robert!" His voice boomed with exaggerated cheer. "Didn't think I'd find you so soon." Robert hesitated only a second before breaking into a smile. "We got you letter but didn't know when you were coming." "Me neither until an hour ago," Albert said, stepping inside uninvited. "Figured I'd drop in, see my big brother and this wonderful family."

Nancy wiped her hands on her apron with a big smile. "Well, you've arrived just in time. Supper's almost ready." Albert's eyes flicked to her, lingering just a fraction too long. Then, he turned toward Becky, and for a moment, she felt his gaze settle on her like a weight pressing down. He gave her a slow nod, unreadable.

Becky looked down at the floor, heart pounding. "Well," Robert said, clapping a hand on Albert's shoulder. "Come in, then. Have some lemonade while we wait to eat." Albert grinned. "Don't mind if I do." He stepped forward, the wooden floor creaking beneath his weight. He removed his hat and tossed it onto the side table, revealing hair that was slicked back, still damp with sweat from the road.

Albert sat with an easy smile, fingers curled around his glass. He was good at this --- playing the part of a long lost relative, slipping seamlessly back into their world. "You're building a life here," he said, glancing around. "Las Vegas suits you."

Robert leaned back in a chair. "Seems so. And you? Ruby Mountains up North? Fur trade? Sounds exciting." "Sure was," said Albert, "but the old Humbolt River ain't what it used to be. Trappin's dryin' up." He didn't want to get too deep in a lie --- he changed the subject. "How are things in Las Vegas?"

Robert sighed, "It's changing fast. The dam's bringing in thousands of workers. Luckily, Uncle Sam is planning an entire city just for them. Boulder City --- no gambling, no liquor. They don't want the workers getting mixed up in all that." Albert raised an eyebrow. "And yet, I imagine plenty of them will still find their way into town."

Becky set the table, trembling as she set each item. Nancy listened in and nodded while finishing the cooking, "The newspaper I work for covers a lot of that. Politicians keep saying they want to keep vice out, but that won't stop workers from heading here on weekends. The city's trying to manage it --- but gambling and drinking have been part of Las Vegas for years. It's not going away."

Robert moved on, "Lucky we have the railroads. They built this town, and now they're keeping it alive. The line's carrying in supplies for the dam --- concrete, steel, machinery --- but it's also bringing in people. Workers, engineers, even tourists. But what happens after the dam's finished? That's what some folks are wondering."

Albert took a slow sip of his lemonade, his mind barely on the conversation. He didn't care about city planning or railroads. He was here for something else. Nancy chimed in with talk of a growing city desperately needing upgraded water and sewer lines and more electricity and housing. Still, he played along, "Sounds like a challenging but exciting time to be in Las Vegas."

When dinner was served, Albert settled into his chair, he stretched out his right hand for some bread, but Becky caught a glimpse of his left --- his deformed hand, the one he always kept curled inward like a claw. He moved it subtly, out of sight, but she knew it was there. She had known it for as long as she could remember.

Albert ate like a wild animal, he always had, consuming large mouthfuls without seeming to even taste or chew. It revolted Becky and brought back disturbing memories in Lincoln. Robert tried to ignore the harsh table manners and asked about Albert's travels. Albert lied cautiously, spinning some tales of life in the wilderness --- trapping beavers in frozen rivers, narrowly escaping a grizzly, trading pelts with rugged mountain men. His voice was smooth, his words practiced, but Becky knew better. She had heard his lies before.

Eventually, the conversation turned back to the dam. Albert was relieved. "They spent a lot of time planning to build the dam in Boulder Canyon, but they made the right choice changing it to Black Canyon," Robert said, cutting into his meat. "I was out there when they scouted it --- solid rock walls, perfect for holding back the river --- a much better choice."

Nodding while swallowing a giant lump of food, Albert said, "And that means more jobs coming in." He leaned back. Robert asked, "That what you're thinking?" Albert grimaced, hoping for pity, "Maybe. The hand don't allow me to do a lotta those jobs, but I hear they need charcoal burners for the mines outside of town. Figured I'd give that a shot."

Becky knew what that meant. Albert was broke. Again. He'd shown up like this in the past --- when he needed something. And just as she expected, before dinner ended, he would charm a promise of money from her father. Almost on cue, Albert said, "Meanwhile, I'm wondering if you might be able to advance a small loan."

Nancy didn't argue. She looked sadly and lovingly at Albert. Becky was revolted. She loved her mother. She admired her smarts and wisdom in life. But how could she be so blind to Albert's manipulation? As the meal wrapped up, Albert leaned back, patting his stomach. "Hell of a meal, Nancy. I'd forgotten how good of a cook you are." Nancy gave a glowing smile. "Of course, darlin' --- I'm so glad you enjoyed it!"

Casually, Albert pushed his chair back and stood. "I won't keep you all. Just wanted to see my family." He glanced at Robert. "We'll talk soon about that loan, okay? Maybe grab a drink?" Robert nodded. "Absolutely." Becky looked down and slumped. Robert too, was being played like a fiddle.

Turning to Becky, his lips curling in something that wasn't quite a smile, Albert said, "Good seeing you again, kid." Becky swallowed hard. "You too." But it was a lie. She never wanted to see him again.

As Albert stepped out into the night, Becky deeply exhaled. Banished memories of a dark night in Lincoln Nebraska, alone with Albert tried to gain re-entry into her head. She tried desperately not to let them back in. After Albert said goodnight, the weight in her chest didn't leave. Because Albert never really left her. And she knew --- he would be back.

Chapter 12: Loss

The days dragged on, but Labor Day finally arrived. Miles was excited for the air show. He seemed excited in general. Was his life actually getting better? He finally beat Joey Franco in the ring and he was going to get a job tomorrow on the Bayonne Bridge. What better way to get out and enjoy what little optimism he had than by going out to see a world of airplanes?

He awoke early that morning and cleaned Max's apartment. He did anything he could think of to keep busy and pass the time. At 11:30 he was on the Fifth Street trolley headed towards the grand hotel at Bergen Point.

The La Tourette was an anomaly in blue collar working-class Bayonne, sitting majestically on the shore of the Kill Van Kull River. Amidst pristinely kept grounds and meticulously manicured shrubbery --- this hotel catered only to the wealthiest, not only in Bayonne, but in all of America.

The Point was hopping when he reached the end of the line. It seemed that all 78,000 residents of Bayonne were filtering onto the grounds of the grand La Tourette. Food smells filled the air --- hot dogs and cotton candy. A brass band played John Phillip Sousa marching music. Parents pushed strollers, kids played chase, elders sat on benches, young couples lay atop their shiny black Model T's looking skyward awaiting the show.

Suddenly, one after another, planes came roaring toward the crowd. Cheers alternated with hushed wonder. Most amazing was when a man actually jumped out of a plane in mid-air, horrifying the crowd until something called a parachute opened and landed him gently on the shore.

There was a lull in the action and Miles started listening to a bickering couple discussing Amelia Earhart's Atlantic Ocean crossing. The wife said, "She's the first woman to fly across the ocean!" But her husband wasn't having any of it. "Not true, all she did was sit in the thing while a man navigated!" Miles laughed, knowing the husband was right. Max taught him well. Earhart did not have the kind of pilot training to make the journey on her own.

In a split second there was no bickering couple, no air show, no La Tourette Hotel. There was only Vanessa Holland, standing 10 yards in front of him. She had perfectly straight blonde hair, soft white shoulders showing outside her dainty colorful sundress, and bright blue eyes he could see from where he was standing. Vanessa had the hand of her little sister, Clarice, helping her manage a cotton candy treat as big as her head.

This was the moment life would change for Miles --- he was finally going to speak to Vanessa Holland! She fixed her hair, looked away and back and smiled. A crowd of people all rushed to see the Velie Monocoupe 70, supposedly flown by Lindbergh himself, which of course held no interest to Miles at the moment. He kept Vanessa in sight.

Finally, he stepped up onto the patio where she and Clarice were standing and came face-to-face with his goddess. She looked at him and smiled, "Hi Miles." Suddenly shy, he panicked. He thought about saying how hot it was today, how impressive the planes were, how pretty she looked, but he couldn't decide! His throat tightened. He coughed, and a large piece of green spittle landed on his hand, in plain sight of Vanessa. He awkwardly wiped it on his hip. Hopelessly embarrassed, he looked down at his feet. "Vanessa," called her father from across the patio, "Come, bring Clarice, there's a clown on the beach." Vanessa turned and walked away with Clarice. Miles couldn't bear to watch.

Miles couldn't move from the spot. Eventually he started shuffling around the grounds. As he stepped into a gazebo overlooking the beach, he spotted Vanessa's sundress. He momentarily thought he could hurry down and try again. But his hopes were instantly crushed when he saw Vanessa laugh and tilt back her head in animated conversation. Jaw clenched and fists tight as iron, Miles watched helplessly. A young man picked a flower from the garden and presented it to her like it was gold. She demurely accepted. Then Vanessa slipped her hand onto Pauley O'Donnell's politely folded arm and they began to stroll.

Chapter 13: The Storm and the Stone

The rain had come suddenly, drenching the desert in a way that felt unnatural. The air had been thick and dry all morning, but by midafternoon, dark clouds had rolled in from the mountains, and the sky had opened up in a torrential downpour.

Robert sat behind the wheel of his truck, gripping it tightly as he navigated the slick, mud-choked road winding through the hills outside of Las Vegas. The water had turned the dust into a thick slick paste, and every turn felt treacherous.

He had been out near the Colorado River, where the government survey teams had started marking the future site of the dam. His work with the road department took him all over the region, and he prided himself on getting to know these roads like the back of his hand. But today, something felt different.

The rain wasn't letting up, and the earth --- so unused to holding water --- was giving way. He could see small rivulets running down the hillsides, carving paths through the loose soil. Rocks had already begun to tumble onto the road in places, forcing him to slow down.

Still, he wasn't worried. Not yet. He reached a sharp bend in the road, flanked by a steep incline on one side and a sheer drop on the other. His tires slipped slightly in the mud as he eased the truck forward. And then --- a sound like thunder, but not from the sky. He looked up just in time to see a mass of rock and earth breaking loose from the hill above. There was no time to react. The boulder --- easily the size of a man --- came crashing down, striking the truck with a force that shattered metal like glass. The vehicle lurched violently, the windshield caving in, and Robert barely had a moment to register the impact before everything went black.

Back at home, Nancy was drying dishes when there was a knock at the door. She had been expecting Robert to return any minute, tracking the storm with concern but trusting in his skill to get home safely. He always did. But when she opened the door, it wasn't Robert standing there. It was one of his coworkers. His face was pale, his hat clutched in both hands. He didn't need to say a word. Nancy knew.

The plate she had been holding slipped from her grasp, shattering on the floor. As much as they had their ups and downs as they struggled through life, she loved Robert. There would be time later for anger --- time to boil and reflect on all her suspicions that Robert's safety supervisors on the job site cared nothing about safety but rather were corrupted by bribes to move the work along at speed to satisfy corporate moguls. For now, she felt only emptiness and loss.

Becky stood with her mother outside in the hot desert sun as they lowered her father's body into the ground. She felt cold, despite the desert heat that had returned in full force now that the storm had passed. People spoke softly, offering condolences, but it all blurred together. The words didn't matter. What mattered was that her father was gone. What mattered was that her mother stood beside her, hollow-eyed and stiff, staring at the grave as though willing Robert to climb back out of it.

But something else also mattered --- a thing that sent icy dread through Becky's veins --- Albert was still here. He stood a few steps away, watching. His feigned expressions of grief nauseated her, especially so, because Albert had already gotten Robert's loan. Albert offered words of comfort to Nancy, even an embrace. But when his eyes met Becky's, she saw something else there. She knew what he was thinking. Robert had been a wall that stood between Albert and what he wanted. Now that wall was gone. And for the first time in her life, Becky felt completely, utterly unprotected.

Chapter 14: Goodbye

Unable to bear the embarrassment of Pauley O'Donnell stepping in on Vanessa Holland's attentions, Miles skipped school. He cringed at the thought of seeing Vanessa again, how she would recall seeing him wiping his hand on his hip. Plus, he needed to show up at the bridge job site today to see Carl whatever-his-name-is. Excited as he was yesterday about this new job, he had a hard time caring now.

Nothing seemed to matter now that he lost Vanessa. But he had to eat. By the time he arrived at the job site, Miles tried to put on a good work face. He hoped he could play the part of an eager young man willing to work.

Carl Callahan's mission in life was to build things and control people. He waived off a handshake offered by Miles. "Yeah, I heard you was comin' today kid. Now lemme tell ya how we do this job. This here's watcha call an arch bridge. We start from both sides and meet in the middle. The ends of one arch gotta be sealed with the next, see? Them arches are getting pretty high up over the water. I got a job for you as a fly-boy. Crane will bring you to the top o' the arch, you'll have ropes around you so you don't fall. Then you and your partner rivet one arch piece to the next."

Petrified at the thought of standing atop the bridge and pale with terror, Miles begged, "Mister Callahan, I can work really hard, nobody works faster and I can carry a ton. But I can't climb up high, it's not something I can do." Callahan was not the kind of man to be compassionate about someone's fears. Impatient, Callahan quipped, "Listen boy, I don't need another God damn driver, loader, or shit shoveler. I got plenty. What I need is a fuckin' fly-boy who ain't afraid of heights. Got it?" Miles couldn't answer. "Get the fuck outta here, I got work to do."

Miles began to drift aimlessly back to Max's apartment. He slumped onto the trolley, took a seat, and stared straight ahead, motionless. His sad desperate thoughts alternated between Vanessa and his empty pockets. The last stop for the Fifth street line was three blocks from Max's apartment. In a few minutes he'd at least be somewhere that felt like home.

But after walking the second block, he found himself approaching a boisterous band of six or eight bouncing youths about his age. As they got closer, he saw it was Pauley O'Donnell's entourage, with Pauley square in the middle. Miles stopped and stood his ground.

"Well, well, look who it is," said Pauley. "This ain't your side of the street, WOP, that's your side," he said pointing across traffic. Miles was in no mood to back down today. Visions of a fresh beating of Joey Franco bolstered his confidence, and rage, fueled by Miles's stinging vision of Vanessa on Pauley's arm, coursed through his veins. The rage felt good. It pushed aside hurt. Miles knew not to let anger get in the way of his focus like he did last time against his orange-haired opponent. This time, he would remain in control. "I'll walk any side I like," he stared. Separating himself from his followers, Pauley walked up to Miles, looking up slightly to meet his eyes, he poked Miles in the chest, "Then how 'bout I just kick your ass on over there," Pauley said. Miles looked back with steely confidence, "bring it boy."

Pauley took a few steps back and started rolling up his sleeves. He circled dramatically to show off for his group of admirers. Miles prepared likewise, hiking up the arms on his tight blue pullover shirt, and taking time to breathe and focus. He began to bounce and send flurries of punches through the hot air in front of him, his usual boxing warm up routine. Pauley kneeled as though he were tying his shoe, but actually he picked up a small handful of sandy pebbles from where the sidewalk met a pathetic strip of grass. Miles entered the imaginary ring, framed by onlookers. Miles knew the group would never violate code and gang up on him. This fight would be one on one.

With perfect boxing form and posture, Miles approached. But this was not a boxing match. Pauley had no intention of following any rules. That was the gym. This was the streets. As Miles got closer, Pauley released the grainy pebbles in Miles's face and disappeared from Miles's view. In a flash, Pauley had dropped down low, hugging both of Miles's knees and driving forward. Churning his legs and driving his shoulders with all his might, Pauley built enough momentum to start Miles moving rapidly backwards. They didn't stop until Miles's back met the unforgiving wall of the building next to them. Upon impact, a mighty grunt came bellowing out of Miles's chest. With polished timing and experience Pauley reached up in perfect synchronization with Miles's body rebounding off the wall. The younger boy grabbed the front of Miles's pullover shirt and pulled sharply downward. Pauley rolled aside so Miles would not fall on top of him.

By the time Miles hit the ground, Pauley was on his feet, ready for the last devastating stage of his assault. A less experienced fighter would have pounced on his prone opponent. But Pauley knew Miles was bigger and stronger and was not yet incapacitated. Miles would have overcome the temporary setback of a fall. Instead, with blinding speed and precision, Pauley reached down to Miles's lower back, slid his hands under Miles's belt, and grabbed tightly around the bottom of the blue pullover. With all the force he had, Pauley pulled the back of the shirt all the way up Miles's back and hooded it over the top of Miles's head, binding his arms in his own clothing. Face down and unable to move his arms, Miles felt the crash of a heavy boot slam into the left side of his rib cage. Before the pain could register, another landed directly into his nose, then again in the same place. From here Pauley could have done anything he wanted to Miles, even kill him.

But Pauley knew the value that his fighting exhibitions provided towards being in charge. He had an audience. For dramatic effect he pulled Miles's head up in a fistful of hair, looked him in the eye, and pointed to the left, "That's your side of the street, boy, go!" Hoisting him to his feet, Pauley ushered his wobbly foe to the curb. "Go I said!" And with a ceremonious kick in the pants, he sent Miles trudging to the other side, blood pouring out of his nose, staining his blue pullover. Pauley's band of merry men rejoiced; Miles slogged the final block to Max's apartment.

Barely able to climb the stairs to Max's flat, Miles stumbled in, nose throbbing, ribs stabbing. But through the pain, Miles sensed something was terribly wrong. He looked over at Max lying on the sofa. Max was not still and peaceful in a quiet alcoholic stupor. He was struggling, eyes bulging, skin bluer than Miles had ever seen. When Max looked over and said, "Hello Miles," Miles knew for sure something was wrong. Miles had never heard Max call him by his real name.

Miles ran to the sofa and kneeled. "Who was it?" asked Max, looking at the blood all over Miles's face and shirt. Not caring and not wanting to talk about it, Miles said, "Pauley." Sucking air, Max said, "Boy's dangerous." "Max I can't work the bridge," said Miles. Max looked up, "It doesn't matter now, you have to leave Bayonne." Miles looked at him, confused, "I can't leave Bayonne, look at you. I gotta take care of you." Max answered, "We don't have much time, Miles. Listen to me. The only way I'm leaving this apartment ever again is feet first, understand? My time is up." Miles looked down, understanding.

"There's too much bad luck here for you and I'm not going to be around to help. I need you to do as I say. I'm not as crazy as you think. I know your name is Miles, Miles Tornero. Butchie was my boy. I'd have been really proud if he grew up like you. I want you to pack up what you have and leave right away. I know it's hot, but take your coat, hat, and gloves. You won't survive without them. Take whatever food we have." He pointed across the room to the tiny randomly-placed furniture piece, "There's $27 over there."

With clarity and precision, Max dutifully continued his final instructions "See this belt? Take yours off and put it on. Always wear it. I cut a slit in it and put a plug of the poison inside. It's behind that piece of duct tape. Someday, you're going to run up against someone you can't fight with your fists. Be careful with it, but remember, it's all about surviving."

Miles did what he was told while Max continued, "Remember the dam we talked about? Find it. It won't be hard. The whole world will be talking about it. Just head West and keep going until it's hotter than hell. Then be smart and survive."

Clothes and food in a pillowcase, money in his pocket, Miles muttered, "I'm afraid Max, I can't leave, I can't leave you." Max looked up, angry. With a massive burst of energy he screamed, "Do it boy!

You hear me? Leave and never look back!" With a final gasp he looked at Miles, "I made a lot of mistakes in my life, but I've never been wrong."

The energy Max spent now drained the tiny man. Even near death, his left leg was furiously bouncing as usual. Breathless, Max stared straight up at the ceiling. Miles stood and bent over and lifted his friend effortlessly in his arms. He carried Max gently to his bed and laid him down, pulling the covers up caringly to his stubbled chin. Max touched Miles's hand, and this time, peacefully whispered, "Go and never look back." Tears streaming down his bloody face, Miles turned and left the apartment for the final time.

Fired from two jobs, failed at love, beaten and humiliated by a younger boy, and now without his only friend in the world, Miles Tornero crossed Avenue E, hopped over the decayed remains of a black German Shepherd next to the railroad tracks, and jumped the back of a Central New Jersey train car.

Section II

Chapter 15: Escape

Miles crouched in the darkness beneath the train trestle, his breath visible in the cold night air. The rails above him groaned as a slow-moving freight train rolled past, the heavy steel wheels grinding against the tracks. He waited for just the right moment. When the last of the boxcars trundled by at a manageable speed, he burst into a sprint, his boots thudding against the ground.

He grabbed the rusted side ladder of a nearby boxcar, gritting his teeth as the cold metal bit into his palms. The train's momentum made the climb a challenge, but he was used to the struggle by now. His muscles screamed in protest, the strain of months spent hopping trains, surviving off scraps, and never quite knowing where he would sleep the next night taking its toll. Yet, despite the exhaustion, he felt the familiar surge of freedom as the train lurched forward, his body thrown into the rhythmic sway of the car's movement. Another night, another journey to another destination unknown, one that could be his last. He tapped his belt for reassurance the poison was still inside.

Miles had heard about "riding the rails" from older men back in Bayonne, but no warning or wisdom could have prepared him for the reality of it. The first time he climbed onto a moving freight train, his heart pounded like a drum against his ribs. He was used to it by now, but it was always terrorizing. He clung to the undercarriage, knees tucked up, every bump in the track rattling his bones. He knew one misstep could send him tumbling beneath the wheels.

At an early stop outside Wheeling, he met an old hobo who looked even older than Max. The older man, weary and wind-worn, tried to school him in survival. "Stay away from the bulls," he warned. "They'll beat your half to death and toss what's left in a ditch." Miles would see it firsthand outside of Ohio. A boy, younger than him, tried to jump a slow-moving train, only for a railroad bull to yank him back down. The boy was kicked so hard in the ribs he couldn't stand. The bull laughed and left him there, wheezing in the dirt.

But the worst sight --- at least so far --- came in a boxcar somewhere around Pittsburgh, where he saw a young man with the "jake leg." The poor soul's feet curled inward, every step a struggle. Other hobos whispered that drinking bootlegged Jamaica Ginger had poisoned his nerves. His legs were ruined, and with them, any chance at work or survival. Miles knew then --- poverty was more than hunger. It was a slow, relentless death. Miles had at least one thing in his favor; seeing this horrific scene, and remembering Max's fate, he would never touch a drop of alcohol. Not to mention, he could never afford, not even for a second, to have the smallest amount of focus taken away from his aim at survival.

As another empty boxcar bumped him along yet another endless journey, the world outside was a blur of dark, rolling landscapes --- fields, forests, and the occasional flicker of distant town lights as the train thundered onward. The wind whipped his face, and the clattering of the train's wheels drowned out everything but the pulse of the rails beneath him. There was no destination that truly mattered, except some faraway place called Las Vegas, where he would find Max's dam.

The life of a hobo was already a thin thread stretched across a yawning gap. A single wrong move --- a missed train, a wrong turn into a bad neighborhood, a run-in with the bulls who patrolled the rails --- could mean an end to everything. There was no safety net, no way to know when the last meal, the last ride, the last moment of peace would come. The world outside, once vast and full of possibility, had started to feel smaller, tighter, more dangerous. But even as Miles wrestled with these thoughts, he kept moving. The rhythmic pulse of the train beneath him was an anchor to his existence. He didn't know where he'd wind up next, but as long he was riding, he still had a chance.

He passed through the long stretches of countryside, its beauty stretching out beneath a glittering blanket of stars. For the first time in as long as he could remember, he felt a quiet sense of belonging --- a rare moment where he wasn't just surviving, but breathing in sync with the land, the rails, and the sound of his own heartbeat. This ride, like many, ended abruptly, another bull, another random escape from an unknown fate.

That was when he saw the campfire. It was a small glow in the distance, nothing more than a flickering orange spot against the endless black. But to Miles, it was a sign. A sign that there were others out here, living on the fringes of society, just like him. Maybe they would have food. Maybe they would have stories. He walked in that direction. He tapped his belt, always a reminder of Max's poison.

A group of men sat huddled around the fire, their faces lined with years of hard living. One was playing a guitar, the soft strumming of the strings carrying into the cool night air. Another, a large man with a rough, weathered face, looked up when Miles approached. "Well, well, what do we have here?" the man said, his voice gravelly. "Just passing through," Miles said, sitting down cautiously. He didn't want to seem too eager. The man studied him for a moment before nodding. "You got food?" Miles shook his head. "No, just water." "Then you're no use," the man muttered, taking a long swig from a bottle. But then he softened. "Ya know what, you look okay kid, come and join us for some Mulligan stew."

Miles had heard about the dish. The name always conjured up a certain charm --- the image of weathered men gathered around a bubbling pot, swapping stories by the firelight under a sprawling, indifferent sky. But the reality was far less poetic. Miles was shocked when he saw the pot --- a desperate, slop-bucket. A grim reflection of the hunger that drove men to scrape together whatever they could find, anything remotely edible --- half rotten potatoes fished from a market's garbage heap, sinewy scraps of meat carved off a long-dead carcass, wilted greens pulled from the roadside, and stale bread crumbled in to thicken the broth, made from water scooped from the sluggish creek he could hear in the distance. Flies swarmed the pot, drawn by the rancid steam curling into the night air. Miles accepted a dented can filled with the slosh and ate gratefully.

For the next few hours, they talked about the journey, about the places they had been, and the hardships they'd endured. Miles listened more than he spoke, grateful for the company, but part of him remained distant --- always watching, always calculating. He had learned the hard way that you couldn't trust anyone fully.

It was late fall of 1929, and groans of the Great Stock Market Crash had begun to spread like an overflowing river across the country. This gave the men something else to talk about; banks failing, companies shuttering, and the nation teetering on the brink of depression. But Miles didn't truly understand much of it. He tried to care, but he couldn't. He never owned anything more than the clothes on his back and the small bundle of necessities that fit in his pack. So, hearing about this "stock market crash," he shrugged. He had nothing. He always had nothing. He had nothing to lose. The news felt like a far-off storm --- something that wouldn't touch him.

When the campfire finally died out and the men began to settle down for sleep, Miles's sharpened instincts told him it was safe to sleep with them. Miles pulled his jacket tighter around his shoulders. His old hat warming his head, his gloves warming his hands, he recalled Max imploring him to take his winter clothes. How right he was, as always. The 27 dollars Max gave him was long gone. But now, as he habitually did, he patted his belt, now cinched a few notches tighter, reassuring himself the poison Max gave him was still in place --- wondering if, or when, he would have to use it.

As the months wore on and the Great Depression thing took hold, something in his chest gnawed at him, a vague unease he couldn't quite shake. The people he met along the way --- seemed to change --- hard men and desperate women, all living hand to mouth, their faces worn with desperation and hardship --- and fears. For the first time, Miles understood that the things he didn't own, the things he had never cared about, were crumbling.

Chapter 16: A New Beginning

Nancy had now been a widow for almost two years, but it still felt like yesterday that she lost Robert. His death had been sudden and brutal, crushed beneath a giant boulder while working on the future highways leading to the Boulder Dam. The officials called it an unavoidable accident, but Nancy knew better. Corners had been cut, safety ignored --- all in the name of speed and profit. Nancy was angry. Robert believed in his work. But the men who controlled the city and the dam project didn't care about workers like Robert, only the money pouring in.

After Robert's death, Nancy had no time for grief. She had Becky to take care of, and in a town like Las Vegas --- booming, corrupt, and run by men who saw women as little more than decoration --- her options were few. At first, she took what work she could, mostly cleaning, bookkeeping, and running errands. But now she was working more and more at The Desert Sun, even though it was on the brink of collapse. It wasn't much better money, but she was passionate about the work.

The paper was run by Henry Calloway, an aging newsman who had been in the business for decades. Unlike the city's larger papers, which were controlled by the elites and filled with bought-and-paid-for stories, The Sun was built on a foundation of truth. Henry was the only journalist in town willing to print the real stories --- the corruption behind the dam contracts, the exploitation of workers, the backroom deals between politicians and businessmen. It had made him many enemies, many of which were able to convince the public that the so-called truth he published was nothing but a bunch of hogwash, calling The Sun the "Las Vegas Rag" whenever they could.

Nancy helped the paper stay afloat. Henry was old, tired, and alone, but he refused to stop fighting. Something in Nancy's sharp mind and unwavering determination caught his attention. She wasn't just working a part-time job --- she had fire in her. She saw the injustice all around her and refused to turn a blind eye, and that was exactly the kind of person Henry needed.

Although she had started off doing small tasks --- copy editing, writing obituaries, and handling bookkeeping, Nancy was now writing real articles. Under Henry's mentorship, she learned the business --- how to track down sources, how to push past intimidation, how to write the truth in a way that couldn't be ignored. The work was dangerous, but Nancy didn't scare easily. Then Henry fell ill.

The doctor said it was his heart, but Nancy suspected it was the weight of too many years spent fighting a battle he knew he was losing. He lasted another six months, guiding Nancy from his chair in the back office, until one evening, he called her in. "I'm not going to make it through the year," he said plainly, never one for dramatics. "And this paper won't either, unless you take it." Nancy was stunned. "Henry, I don't have the money..." "I'm not asking for money," he cut in. "I'm asking you to keep it alive." It wasn't a gift --- it was a challenge. He wasn't offering charity; he was offering responsibility. A week later, Henry was gone.

Nancy inherited The Desert Sun and poured everything she had into it. But it wasn't just about keeping a business running --- it was about carrying on a mission. She refused to let the truth die with Henry, and she refused to let the powerful men in Las Vegas silence the voices of the people. Part of her drive came from a need to do what was right --- and part came from wanting to somehow avenge Robert's unnecessary death.

Big Business in the city fought her at every turn. The bigger papers --- The Silver Star and The Gazette --- mocked her, calling The Desert Sun a widow's vanity project. Business owners, afraid of retaliation, were reluctant to advertise with her. And then there were the veiled threats --- little mentions here and there by powerful people that she was getting too big for her britches --- and ought to be careful. Even Mayor Wallace, popular and congenial, but secretly aligned with every elite in the town, would politely approach Nancy at town meetings and other public events and subtly but clearly let her know that overstepping would have "consequences."

She kept going. One afternoon, as she and Becky walked through the streets of downtown Las Vegas, they passed by The Silver Star's office. A reporter stood outside, speaking with a well-dressed man Nancy recognized --- Clifford Graves, one of the city's most powerful land developers. "The railroad's progress has been outstanding," the reporter said, voice full of rehearsed admiration. "A real boost to our economy. The workmen are moving fast --- thanks to the leadership of Mr. Graves. A true visionary."

Nancy clenched her jaw. She knew the truth. Graves had been stealing land from small-time owners for years, using legal loopholes and outright threats to push them off their property. He wasn't a visionary --- he was a crook. But no one would dare print that, because he had the money to make sure they didn't. That was the kind of power Nancy was up against.

But Nancy and Becky weren't entirely alone. Becky had always been active in their church --- a modest but tight-knit congregation that believed in honesty, hard work, and looking out for one another. Every Sunday, Becky sat in the front row, soaking in the sermons about standing up for what was right, about truth and justice. The pastor's wife, Mrs. Ellison, took a special liking to her and soon let Becky help with organizing events, managing donations, and even reading scripture aloud. It was through the church that The Desert Sun found its first real supporters.

Becky, eager to help her mother, started mentioning the paper in conversation. She told the women at Sunday gatherings about the stories they were printing --- the real stories. She spoke to families who had lost fathers and brothers to dangerous working conditions, who had been ignored by the bigger newspapers. She helped distribute copies at church events, slipping them into the hands of people who were beginning to realize they weren't alone in their struggles. The churchgoers, bound by faith and trust in one another, began to see The Desert Sun as more than just a newspaper. It was a beacon of truth in a city filled with corruption. Her fellow parishioners believed in it, they spread the word.

Nancy started noticing new faces coming into the shop, people who wanted to buy copies, who whispered their support, who slipped her stories about the things the bigger papers wouldn't print. It wasn't much, but it was a start. Later that night, Becky sat across from her mother at their small wooden table, twirling a strand of her hair. "Mama, do you ever think we'll be able to get ahead?" Nancy looked at her daughter, seeing the same fire she once had. "We might not have money, and we might not have power," she said. "But we have the truth. And as long as I'm breathing, we're going to tell it."

Chapter 17: Manhood

Direction was a relative term on the rails. Hopefully it was West --- at least most times --- with any luck. Other times it was wherever safety --- or chance --- pointed. Miles didn't know much geography, especially not stuck in nowhere without a map. He knew enough to know that Michigan and Texas were not on the way to Las Vegas, but he'd already been to both. In Texas, way longer than he wanted to be, thanks to an angry Sheriff who didn't care much for "folks not around these parts."

Now, he wasn't sure where he was --- but it was warm, and quiet, and seemingly safe. There was a heavy scent of pine and the sound of crickets. Miles stood and waivered a bit --- the weight of yet another journey settling deep in his bones. With repetition a routine part of his travels, Miles would often lose track of time --- saved only by an occasional random newspaper he'd find along the way. He'd seen much, survived much, but there was a quiet hollowness in him now, a need for something more than the endless ride westward. The journey so far had hardened him. But he needed to rest, recuperate, before he could move safely on.

That was when he came across the widow's farm. It wasn't much, just a small plot of land with a modest home, nestled against a backdrop of dry hills and a smattering of pine trees. Miles had been riding the rails for many months by this point, and his body had begun to feel every minute of it. A bed, a meal, even a moment of peace, seemed like fantasies. When the widow saw him walking up the road, she didn't hesitate to offer him work. Hannah was a solitary woman, with a heavy German accent. She was strong and thick but perfectly proportioned, a perfect warrior woman had she lived in another time. There was something in her eyes that told Miles she wasn't afraid of much. "You look like you could use some food," she said, her voice disciplined and deliberate. "And some work. I could use an extra hand."

Miles hesitated for a moment, but the hunger gnawing at his stomach outweighed any caution. He nodded, grateful for the chance, and followed her into the small house. The kitchen smelled of baked bread and warm stew, a scent that made his stomach growl louder. He ate his fill that evening, and as the night wore on, Hannah told him about her life on the farm --- how she'd lost her husband years ago, how she'd learned to survive on her own. She had a quiet strength about her, a resilience that spoke to the harshness of the land and the solitude she had embraced.

Over the next few months, Miles worked harder than he ever had before. He fixed fences, cleaned the barn, tended to animals, and even helped with planting a small vegetable garden. It wasn't glamorous work, but it was honest, and for the first time in a long while, Miles felt useful. The widow was kind but firm, and as time passed, he began to feel a sense of purpose that had been missing from his life for so long.

One evening, after a long day in the fields, Hannah invited him inside for a drink. She poured two glasses of bootleg whiskey, her movements slow but sure. Miles passed on the liquor --- a vivid image of Max's ravaged body shot through his head --- but accepted some tea, grateful for the warmth it offered against the evening chill. The fire crackled in the hearth, casting flickering shadows on the walls as they talked about everything and nothing. Age defied Hannah, old expressions, youthful body. She spoke of the past, of the land, and of the world outside her small farm, and Miles listened, his mind a little clearer from the tea, and hers a bit freer with each sip of the whiskey.

Later that night, as the fire burned low, the conversation shifted. Hannah, perhaps feeling empowered by a drink or two, looked at him differently. There was a moment, an undeniable shift in the air, as if the space between them had shrunk to nothing. She reached for his hand, her touch surprisingly soft for a woman who had worked the land all her life. Her eyes searched his, and in that moment, Miles saw something in her gaze --- something deep and unspoken. "You're a man now," she said, her voice low. "You need to understand what it means to be with a woman."

Miles didn't know what to say, didn't know what to feel. He had never been with a woman --- and Hannah could tell. But she didn't wait for an answer. Her lips met his in a kiss that was both tender and knowing, a kiss that spoke of years of solitude but also of a compassionate soul. It was different from what he had imagined, different from the restless urges he had once carried as a boy. Hannah was reassuring, comforting. She guided him. "Slowly," she said. "Always slowly, like this." There was something honest in it, something grounding. She led him gently, her hands guiding him in a way that was both nurturing and forceful, teaching him more than he had ever learned in any other place.

The night passed. He awoke alone in his own bed. Miles knew he had learned something crucial. It wasn't just about the physical act --- it was about understanding what it meant to share intimacy, to give and to receive, to connect with someone beyond the surface. Hannah entered his room as nothing had happened the night before, and greeted him platonically, and dutifully, with purpose. She knew he had to move on. "It's time," she said. Miles noticed all his belongings, and freshly laundered clothes, all neatly held in Hannah's arms.

His time at Hannah's revived him --- built him --- his frame no longer boyish --- months of digging and heavy lifting sculpted his body, arms like chiseled steel, chest as broad and solid as the barn doors he passed through every day. When he left Hannah, he was a bigger man --- outside and in. But the lessons of that night stayed with him, echoing in the back of his mind as he continued his journey westward. There were still many miles to go, many hardships to endure. But now, he knew better how to handle himself with women, how to be a man. He tapped his belt, and moved on to more unknown.

Chapter 18: The Favor

The morning was already hot when Nancy stepped out of her small office. She couldn't escape the searing sun overhead, but she had learned to ignore it. Life in Las Vegas was like that --- constant heat, harsh realities, and the ever-present hum of industry in the background. The Desert Sun had become her anchor. The paper was still small, but it was growing, and its loyal followers loved the truth it delivered. Nancy had made sure of that, cutting through the veils of lies and half-truths that most others peddled. But the more it grew, the more intolerant the elites of the city became.

Her routine had become a kind of armor. She woke early, brewed coffee, sifted through the letters and advertisements, and then headed out to meet with business owners to write her articles. They were simple pieces, spotlighting the people who made this town work. But it was the truth they told that resonated with the public. The community was thirsty for honesty.

Today, she had an appointment at the Ice House. The factory was an unusual feature in the desert, an oasis of chilled perfection in the middle of heat. Nancy had heard of it from a few local customers who had praised its operation, how they sourced their ice from frozen lakes far out of town, how they had mastered the science of refrigeration, and how their products were essential to the town's many speakeasies and hotels. She was eager to meet the owner and feature this interesting business in The Sun.

As she walked into the Ice House, the cool air hit her like a blast of refreshment. She was greeted by a distinguished man, tall, dark, sleek, muscular, with a confident, almost effortless air about him. His hair was dark and slicked back, a slight curl at the nape of his neck. He wore a linen shirt, sleeves rolled up, revealing forearms etched with the kind of muscles that spoke of hard work. His eyes were a deep, intense brown, the kind of eyes that could hold you captive. "You must be Nancy," he said with a smile. "I'm Charlie McCormick. Welcome to the Ice House." Nancy extended her hand, feeling a spark as his fingers brushed hers. "Thank you for taking the time to show me around, Mr. McCormick."

He chuckled softly, a hint of something magnetic in his voice. "Charlie, please. It's not often we get to meet someone who appreciates what we do here, especially not someone as lovely as you." Nancy really never stopped to realize that her stunning good looks had remained through many harsh years --- they never seemed to matter. "Not many people understand how much goes into making ice available in the desert," Charlie said. He gestured to a man nearby, "This is Andy. He's been working here for years, helps me with everything." Andy gave a friendly wave and joked, "He means the other way around. Charlie helps me with everything." Nancy was impressed; a manger who ran a tight ship but also allowed friendly banter with his staff. Charlie added, "And this here is Bud, ready for a delivery. That big leather pad on his shoulder protects him from the ice he'll be hauling on it. And those tongs can handle a 50-pound block." Bud tipped his hat, "Pleased to meet you ma'am."

They began the tour, and Charlie's knowledge was impressive. He spoke with authority, explaining the delicate process of ice-making, how they brought the ice in large blocks from lakes further north, how it was carefully stored and sliced for different purposes --- restaurants, hotels, and, of course, the speakeasies. He even took her into the back room where enormous blocks of ice were stacked, the air thick with the scent of cold.

As they walked, Nancy found herself drawn to his easy manner and sharp wit. He wasn't like the men she was used to dealing with --- calculating, cynical, and looking for something from her. No, Charlie seemed different. He was strong, grounded, and a bit charming in a way that made Nancy feel like she could drop her guard. She hadn't felt that way in years. At the end of the tour, they stood in the front of the Ice House, the afternoon sun casting long shadows. Nancy had her notebook out, ready to take her final notes. "I have to admit, this place is fascinating," she said. "I had no idea how much work goes into producing something as simple as ice in a town like this."

Charlie smiled again, his lips curling just slightly. "It's a labor of love. We've been doing this for years, and it's the heart of the town, even if most people don't see it." Nancy nodded, tapping her pen against her notebook. "You've definitely earned your place in this town's history. I'm excited to write about it."

"And I'm glad you'll be writing about us," Charlie said, his voice low. "If you need anything more for the article, I'd be happy to help. And..." He paused, his gaze meeting hers with a sudden intensity. "I was wondering if I could take you out sometime. After all, I think the Ice House owes you a drink for that article."

Nancy hesitated for a moment, then gave a teasing smile. "Are you sure you want to do that, Mr. McCormick? I mean, let's be clear: anything I write about this place has nothing to do with anything personal between us, alright? This article will be all about the Ice House, just as I see it, not how you want me to see it." Charlie's lips twitched, as though he was amused by her carefulness. "Fair enough. No funny business."

She crossed her arms. "And, I suppose, a man of your caliber, willing to win the interest of a lady such as me, might be willing to do me a small favor if you're really that interested." His eyebrows raised in curiosity. "A favor? What kind of favor?" Nancy smiled, her tone light but serious. "Maybe more than a small favor. Are you game?"

Charlie seemed to think for a moment before nodding. "Whatever it is, I'd be glad to do it." With pleasantries and flirtations skillfully placed by both sides, they began a polite departure. "I'll be in touch," said Nancy. She didn't know what favor she might need, but there was something protective about him, which could come in handy. If nothing else, it was a good test. He passed.

As Charlie made his way out of the Ice House, Nancy turned and glanced over her shoulder. She felt a subtle shiver crawl up her spine, the hairs on the back of her neck prickling. Was she being watched? Out of the corner of her eye, she caught sight of him: Albert, standing across the street. But by the time her head turned towards him, he had quickly averted his stare, looking down to kick a few stones on the ground. Then, just as quickly, he turned and disappeared into the shadows of the bustling street.

Nancy's brow furrowed, assuming he hadn't seen her. 'That's odd,' she thought. She realized now that she'd only seen Albert a few times since he visited when Robert was still alive, but she couldn't even recall when --- it was a long time. But, smitten with her witty repartee with Charlie, she dismissed Albert's appearance as just a coincidence. After all, she knew he worked on the edge of town now, and why shouldn't he be seen here or there?

As she turned back to Charlie, he gave a friendly wave. 'Perfect,' she thought.

Chapter 19: The Mule

It was the heat that first brought them together, the desert sun beating down relentlessly on the two men as they both sought cover beneath the same scrap of railroad debris. Miles had been riding the rails for month, making his way West toward the promise of Las Vegas, but he hadn't met anyone yet who seemed as resilient to the harshness of the world as Billy. They had both been running, though for different reasons. Billy was a former lumberjack from Vermont, just as scrappy and wild as Miles, but there was an unmistakable power in his eyes --- one that spoke of a man who may have been broken by life but capable of building it back better than before.

When they met, Miles was crouched low in a hobo camp, nursing a small fire he'd kindled with bits of broken crates. Billy came up from behind, his silhouette outlined against the setting sun. His face was rough, eyes hidden beneath the brim of a weathered hat, but there was no mistaking trust in his eyes.

"Got a light?" Billy's voice was light, upbeat, the kind that matched the an oddly happy appearance. Miles didn't hesitate. "Sure." He passed the matchbook over without a word, and soon, Billy had a smoke hanging from his lips, eyes friendly, even through a plume of smoke. Nonetheless, Miles tapped his belt. He always tapped his belt.

They didn't exchange many words at first, but Miles could sense that Billy was sizing him up, the same way a man would when looking at a possible ally --- or a threat. There was a moment of silence as the two men shared a knowing glance. They both knew what it was like to travel alone, but neither of them seemed particularly interested in doing it anymore.

Billy threw a small rock into the fire, his gaze fixed on the flickering flames. "Where you headed?" "Las Vegas," Miles answered. He didn't know why he told Billy the truth --- there wasn't much reason for it, not in this life. But something about Billy felt trustworthy, even if he didn't fully understand why. Billy took a long drag from his cigarette and exhaled slowly, his eyes flicking from the smoke to Miles. "What's waiting for you there?" Miles hesitated, "Survival." Billy nodded as if that was the only answer that mattered. "Me too," he said. "Got no family, no home. Hell, got nothing but my hands and what I can scrape together." They briefly exchanged biographies. As short as possible. They didn't need to know much. Billy was a lumberjack from Vermont, looking for a better life. Miles was vaguer. Working at a men's clothing store didn't sound so good compared to being a lumberjack. "Worked building a bridge in Bayonne," he lied.

They shared a quiet understanding in that moment, an unspoken bond forming between them. For the next month or so, they traveled together, surviving on the edges of society, hopping trains and sneaking through towns. They spent their nights under bridges, in fields, and in the corners of abandoned buildings, and, of course, on railroad cars, always on the lookout for bulls --- the railroad security officers who brutally hunted down and punished anyone caught riding the rails without permission.

It was during their last escape that the two of them found themselves running for their lives. They had snuck onto a slow-moving freight train, the kind that lumbered through vast open spaces, carrying its cargo across miles of barren land. They were huddled in a hidden spot behind crates when a pair of bulls appeared at the end of the train. They didn't hesitate. It was clear they had been looking for them the whole time.

Billy's eyes flashed with alarm as the bulls approached, and he grabbed Miles's arm. "Move!" he shouted, his voice urgent. They bolted from the train, leaping off the back and hitting the ground with a practiced bouncing roll they had each learned from previous escapes. This time, surprisingly, the bulls pursued.

Miles's legs burned as they ran, pushing faster than ever before, the sound of heavy boots pounding behind them. They ducked behind a mound of sand as the bulls passed by, narrowly escaping their grasp. But the relief didn't last long. The bulls circled back, and Miles and Billy knew they couldn't outrun them much longer. "That way!" Billy hissed, pointing to a thicket of brush nearby. They veered off course, hoping to throw the bulls off their trail, but the two of them were barely holding it together, sweat soaking their clothes, feet aching, and their hearts pounding in their chests. The bulls abandoned chase --- finally. Miles and Billy were spent.

It was then, as they cut through the brush, that they saw it --- a lone mule, grazing near the edge of a dried-up riverbed. The mule didn't seem startled, as if it had been abandoned by its owner. Its coat was dusty, its body thin, but it was alive. And as they neared it, the mule lifted its head, ears flicking nervously in their direction.

Billy eyed the animal warily. "Mule," he muttered. "Probably a stray." Miles was too winded to speak. Billy's usual friendly eyes turned grim. As hunger twisted their bellies, there was a brief, brutal silence between them. They both understood the inevitable. They needed the mule to survive.

They had spent too many days on the brink of starvation, but the reality of what they were about to do --- what they had to do --- was another kind of brutality. His mind wandered back to his time on the rails, to the people he had met along the way, the stories of hunger and death that hung around the hobo camps like a thick fog. But none of those stories had prepared him for this moment.

Billy took the reins and calmed the mule. "Shh," Billy whispered, almost as if speaking to the mule in the same gentle tone he might've used with a child. His eyes flickered to Miles, swallowed hard. "How... do we..." "Rocks," Billy cut him off. "No choice." Billy nodded to one of many nearby.

Miles knew what he had to do. Reluctantly, but with purpose, he raised the stone. He knew he must be fast. He knew he had only one easy chance. While Billy continued to whisper, Miles crashed the heavy mass into the animal's skull. Dust flew. No blood. The mule screamed an eerie sound and kicked its back legs with all its might. Disoriented the mule crashed to ground. Before it could rise, Miles smashed again. Billy grabbed a smaller rock with one hand and flung it full force into the animal's face. The blows were not enough to silence the beast. Minutes passed like hours as they pounded --- over and over --- almost praying that this strike would be the final strike.

Exhausted, they knelt beside the motionless mule, their next task no less gruesome. They used jagged ends of large stones to crack open its flesh. The blood began to congeal, slowly turning black in the heat of the desert sun. They worked in silence, their hands slick with fluid, sweat trickling down their faces as they carved out the meat from the mule's body. The smell was overpowering, thick and foul, but hunger pounded their bodies like the same rocks that pounded the mule. They didn't stop, didn't pause to consider the horror of what they were doing. They just kept working, the sound of bone cracking echoing in the vast emptiness around them.

Finally, they had enough. Billy started a small fire, the dry brush crackling as they prepared the meat. They roasted it, turning it over the fire until it was charred and dark, the smell of cooking flesh mingling with the acrid air of the desert. When it was done, they didn't speak. There was no need. There seemed nothing human to say.

Miles ate slowly at first, barely tasting the meat as he chewed. His mind swam in a haze of exhaustion and shock, the rawness of the moment settling heavily on his shoulders. Every bite seemed to strip away a little more of his humanity, but he knew there was no other choice. They couldn't afford weakness. Not now. Billy ate with a kind of dark determination, his eyes distant, his mind clearly elsewhere as he tore into the mule's flesh. Miles watched him for a moment before looking away, focusing on his own desperate task at hand.

The sun sank lower in the sky, casting long shadows across the desert floor as they sat in silence, both men too tired to even move. Their bodies were raw and battered, their spirits hanging by a thread, but they had made it. They had found a way to survive.

As the fire slowly died, the two men sat beside it, broken. Miles stared into the flames, his mind a swirl of thoughts. He could barely process it all --- the brutal journey, the death of the mule, the hunger that had pushed them to the brink of insanity. But they were still alive. That was what mattered now. "We'll make it," Billy said after a long silence. His voice was hoarse, but there was something steady in it.

They awoke the next morning and began walking. Gradually things changed. Signs of civilization. A sign, a paved road in the distance, an old car darting across it. Miles's heart dropped and danced at the same time. After more than two years of riding the rails, he realized, though barely standing, he was finally entering Las Vegas.

Chapter 20: Fighting Fire with Fire

Nancy had always known she was taking a risk by publishing the truth. From the moment she took over The Desert Sun, she understood that exposing the corruption of the city's elite would make her powerful enemies. Looks and comments she received at town meetings were becoming more direct, less subtle. The mayor seemed a bit less pleasant --- even though his past pleasantries were easily seen as thinly veiled threats. The stakes seemed to be rising.

It started with Becky's worry over her friend Belinda. The two girls had met while working at a dress shop, stitching hems and chatting about their dreams for the future. Belinda had a quick wit and a warm heart, but she also had a troubled past. Her father had disappeared when she was young, and her mother --- exhausted and broken by years of hard living --- had taken to the bottle, leaving Belinda, beautiful but vulnerable in every way, to fend for herself with little guidance.

Then, suddenly, Belinda was gone. No notice, no explanation. Becky hoped to find her at the home with Belinda's single room inside, a common way of living in 1930's Las Vegas, as homeowners in the burgeoning city made ends meet by petitioning small rooms in their house. No luck. She checked the shops where she sometimes worked odd jobs, and even inquired at the church. Nothing. She knew something was wrong, and when she told Nancy, her mother saw the deep worry in her daughter's eyes.

Nancy began asking questions, visiting a variety of establishments throughout the town, the Apache Hotel, the Las Vegas Pharmacy, the shop where Belinda had last worked. Nothing. Then, in Anderson Grocery, she overheard whispers at the market about Belinda's possible temptation to the edges of Las Vegas's tawdry street life. Eventually, the truth revealed itself in fragments. A name came up --- a man named Mr. Finch, a well-known figure in the city's nightlife, who operated The Pair-O-Dice out on Highway 91. More than a place for drinking and gambling, the establishment had a darker reputation as a gateway into something far worse. Nancy knew what that meant.

And she knew she had to act. Armed with her camera and a fabricated story about writing a piece on the city's growing nightlife, Nancy gained entry to the club --- followed distantly by a hooded man, deliberately hiding his face. The dimly lit room pulsed with jazz, cigarette smoke, and the scent of whiskey. She had dressed carefully --- not too flashy, but refined enough to blend in. The hooded man stayed an awkward distance away, watching but appearing disengaged. A man in a pressed suit, clearly the establishment's owner, greeted her with a slick smile.

"A newspaper lady," Finch said smoothly. "You want to write about our little slice of paradise?" Nancy returned his smile, playing the role she needed to. "Absolutely. I've heard this is one of the finest places in town, and my readers want to know what makes it so special." The owner laughed, pleased with himself, "You came to the right place."

He led her through the main floor, past men in tailored suits tossing dice, women draped in silk and pearls sipping gin from delicate glasses. Nancy listened carefully, noting the faces, the laughter that sounded just a little too forced. But she was here for something else --- something darker. Through a side door, a hallway stretched deeper into the building, where the real business was conducted. Nancy knew she had to be careful. With a glance around, she made an excuse --- mentioning the powder room --- slipped away when no one was watching --- except the hooded man who followed behind her.

She moved quickly down the hallway, passing doors with muffled voices behind them, her heart pounding. Finally, she heard a familiar voice. Belinda. Nancy peeked through a cracked doorway and saw her --- a pale and trembling Belinda perched on the edge of a velvet-covered bed. Across from her, half undressed, was none other than Mayor Wallace. Nancy's stomach turned. This was worse than she had imagined.

She steadied herself, then acted fast. She pushed the door open and stepped inside, camera raised. The flash exploded in the dimly lit room, capturing the stunned face of the mayor as he fumbled to cover himself. Then another. And another. "What the hell..." he sputtered. Nancy's voice was cold and firm. "She is off limits. My daughter is off limits. I am off limits. And my business is off limits." She spoke firmly, deliberately. "Do you understand me?"

Belinda gasped, unable to understand what was happening. The mayor's face turned beet red as he yanked his trousers back into place. He was clearly no longer in the position of power he usually held over Nancy at town meetings. Looking from Nancy to Belinda and back again, he knew there was no escaping this. If she published these photos, his career --- and his carefully built reputation --- would be in ruins. He swallowed hard. "Yes," he whispered, barely audible. Nancy could not resist turning the tables with one more stab, one she'd had to endure on many an occasion. "You do understand there will be 'consequences,' yes?" Wallace answered sheepishly, "Yes. I understand."

Nancy lowered the camera but kept her sharp gaze on him. "Good. Because if I so much as feel a threat toward me or my family or my business, these pictures will find their way into every home in Las Vegas. And trust me, Mr. Mayor, no amount of bribery or backroom dealing will make them disappear."

The mayor's shoulders sagged. He knew he was beaten. Nancy turned to Belinda and took her hand. "Let's go, sweetheart." Belinda clung to Nancy as they stepped out of the room and into the night. "Oh," she said to the mayor, "If you have any thoughts of overpowering me and taking my camera, this gentleman behind me may have some objections." The short chubby mayor glanced in the direction where Nancy pointed, noticing a hulking hooded man, face unseen, in the shadows of the hallway. Charlie was pleased to make good on his favor.

The next morning, Nancy went into the office. Something was amiss. Drawers opened, everything a mess. She shouted aloud to no one, "son of a bitch," and made an instant beeline to the mayor's office. Barging past the receptionist, she blasted into his office. "You idiot," she screamed. "Do you think I'd be stupid enough to hide the photographs that carelessly?" He sat silent, embarrassed. "Let me be clear," those photos will never be seen by anyone until I want them to be seen. And if you make me disappear, they will surface anyway. Do you understand?" "Understood," he said. Little did he know, the photos were safely iced away in a different way --- almost literally on ice --- another favor from Charlie.

"And two more things," she said. "First, the girl gets a real job on the city payroll starting tomorrow. She will be in your office tomorrow afternoon. Make sure you're not there and somebody else handles the hiring. Second, that job opening for a secretary at the dam employment office --- it goes to my daughter --- immediately --- understood?" "Yes," he said. From this moment on, Nancy was untouchable. She had fought fire with fire. And won.

Chapter 21: From Hell to Hell

Miles and Billy staggered on the dust-choked streets on the outskirts of Las Vegas, blood from the mule still covered their clothes. Their legs heavy and uncooperative, Bodies so tired that each step felt like a battle. He and Billy approached as two ragged figures, barely recognizable as men after months of living on the rails, their clothes frayed and their faces drawn with exhaustion. The blistering desert sun made their already brutal journey feel endless. But the faint hope of work on the Boulder Dam kept them going, kept them moving forward even when their bodies screamed in protest.

For the last few days, harshly-cooked mule meat, now dried and stinking in their pockets, had been the only thing keeping them alive. They killed the mule out of desperation, after their hunger had shaped them into something primal. Remnants of it, greasy and chewy, clung to the fabric of their shirts and the tips of their fingers. They were on the verge of collapse when they finally spotted the distant outline of the city. Billy muttered something about the dam, but Miles barely heard, his thoughts a haze of thirst and fatigue.

They entered like two ghosts, not knowing what awaited them or where to turn. The town had changed since they'd heard rumors about the booming construction. But what they didn't know --- what no one had warned them about --- was the desperate, raw reality of the "Hoovervilles," sprung up randomly and seemingly everywhere in the burgeoning railroad town --- shanty towns named in mock honor of the President of the country, thousands of miles away. Miles and Billy were not the only desperate souls descending on the area.

"Let's find somewhere to rest," Billy said, his voice rough with exhaustion. "No sense in rushin' in like cattle. We gotta stick together."

Miles nodded as the sun started setting, the shadows growing long and eerie in the dry heat. As the city began to flicker to life around them, a small crowd began to form along the outskirts of town. Shuffling men and women, all with the same hollow-eyed look, their movements slow, deliberate, and uncertain. Men in tattered clothes sat on the edges of makeshift fire pits, their faces half-hidden under dirty hats or stained bandanas. There were families too, but they huddled together in groups, staying close to their lean-to shacks of scrap metal and cardboard.

"You reckon this is it?" Billy asked, wiping his brow and squinting at the crowd. "I'm thinkin' we'd better head to the dam site before it's all spoken for." But Miles wasn't sure. He felt the air change, thick with something he couldn't name --- danger? Or was it just the weight of hopelessness, hanging like a fog in the city's heart? Whatever it was, it pressed in on him, making his chest tight. The town felt like a trap. Insecure, Miles tapped his belt. The poison was still there.

Before Miles could respond, the sound of a harsh voice cut through the air. "You there!" someone shouted. A large, wiry man, his face slick with sweat, approached them. "You got any work for today, or are you just another pair of hobos lookin' for handouts?" Billy straightened up, instinctively putting a hand to his pocket where the last of the mule meat was hidden. "Just looking for a place to sleep, partner. We're on our way to the dam." "Dam's closed for business if you ain't got yourself some work," the man sneered. "That's what they all say. Everyone's tryin' to get in. Ain't no jobs for a pair of bums like you."

Billy's temper flared. "I'm no bum, mister. You best keep your mouth shut if you ain't got anything useful to say." The man didn't back down. Instead, he glanced at Miles with an odd, calculating look before he pointed toward a clearing, where several men gathered around a fire. "You might want to talk to Mac. He runs things around here." Billy shot a quick look at Miles. "We stick together, yeah?" "Yeah," Miles agreed, though he didn't fully trust the man. Something about the way the man's eyes flickered made him uneasy.

The two of them walked toward the clearing, the heavy silence between them punctuated only by the shuffle of boots on gravel. As they neared the fire, the men stared at them, sizing them up as though they were fresh meat. Billy took a step back, his expression tight with distrust. Miles followed suit, but the unease in his gut was now accompanied by a deep sense of foreboding.

Then, without warning, the crowd erupted into a flurry of motion, the fire crackling louder as people scrambled to make way. Billy grabbed Miles by the arm. "We gotta get outta here," he whispered harshly. "This is no place for us." But before they could retreat, chaos struck. A sharp, shrill voice pierced the air. "They got food! The bastards have food!" A man lunged at them, his face contorted in hunger and madness.

Miles barely saw it coming, the movement too quick to react. Billy shoved him aside, and the next thing Miles knew, he was on the ground, the weight of the hungry mob pushing against him. He couldn't breathe, couldn't see. The roar of voices was deafening, and the smell of sweat and desperation mixed with the foul stench of the mule meat.

Then, just as quickly as it had started, it ended. The man who had attacked them was pulled away, the mob retreating to their places around the fire. Miles lay there for a moment, dazed and shaken, before he scrambled to his feet. Billy was gone. Billy had vanished, swallowed up by the same desperation that consumed the rest of the men in this place. Miles's heart pounded in his chest as he looked around, but there was no sign of his friend. No trace.

In that moment, Miles realized he was alone again, alone in a city that felt like a cage. No railcars to ride, no familiar faces to cling to.

He was just another face in the crowd of broken men and women who had come to Las Vegas hoping to build something, only to be ground down by the same forces that had torn their lives apart.

He swallowed hard, knowing that his journey was far from over, but now, it was something more than just survival. It was about proving he could make it, no matter how hard it got. And for that, he would have to join the ranks of the broken, the ones who had no choice but to survive. With a sigh, Miles tapped his belt, a habit now, knowing the poison was still inside, and set off deeper into Hooverville, knowing he had to once again survive in a world of desperation.

Chapter 22: No Surprise

Becky adjusted the collar of her blouse, the only decent one she owned, and stared at her reflection in the small, cracked mirror propped against the wall of their cramped apartment. The desert light filtered through the tattered curtains, casting streaks of gold across the room. Today was the day. A real job --- a steady paycheck. The security she and her mother had desperately needed for so long.

Nancy stood behind her, arms crossed, watching with a mix of pride and something else --- relief, maybe, but also unease. "Sweetheart," she said, reaching out to fix a stray curl behind Becky's ear. "I remember it like it was only yesterday when you were just a little girl in the back seat when we first drove out here. Now look at you --- 18 years old, all grown up. I'm so proud of you sweetheart. Just keep your head down, do your work, and don't let those men think you're just some pretty face behind a desk." Nancy knew that if any man so much as looked at Becky sideways, she'd be all over the mayor in a second --- still, there was always the possibility.

Becky smiled. "Okay, Mama." Nancy exhaled and turned away, busying herself with a stack of newspapers on the kitchen table, though Becky knew her mother's mind was elsewhere. Nancy had fought for this job --- leveraged the mayor's tawdry secret --- but Becky didn't need to know. The employment office was not run by the city, but in a town like Las Vegas, power wasn't always in official titles. It was in the favors people owed and the dirt people had on each other. And Nancy had dirt. Enough to ensure her daughter got the secretary position, no questions asked.

Becky put on a few finishing touches, feeling the weight of the morning settle on her shoulders. She had worked before --- small jobs, unreliable and underpaid, just enough to keep food on the table and the lights flickering. But this... this was different. This was a position people envied. The men standing outside the employment office every morning, desperate for a shot at working on the dam, would see her walking in through the front doors, past them, with a job already secured. The thought made her proud but uneasy.

She stepped outside into the heat, her shoes kicking up dust along the uneven path toward the main part of town. Nancy followed her to the door but didn't step out. "You come straight home after work, Becky," she warned. "And if anyone gives you trouble, you come to me." Becky turned, her smile soft but sure. "I will, Mama."

The employment office was already bustling when she arrived. The sun had barely begun its ascent, but the air was thick with the smell of unwashed bodies, desperation, and the ever-present dust that settled into every crevice of the city. A crowd of men gathered outside, hopeful laborers waiting for their numbers to be called. The process was simple --- names and numbers on a list, a man stepping onto the back of a truck, bound for the dam site or back to waiting another day.

Becky had never been inside the office before, but as she stepped through the door, she felt the weight of eyes on her. Not just the desperate stares from the men outside, but the workers inside. She was new. A girl in a man's world. "Ah, the new girl," a voice called from the side. Becky turned to see a tall, wiry man with slicked-back hair and a cigarette dangling from his lips. Becky squared her shoulders. "Becky McGuire," she said, keeping her voice steady.

The man grinned and nodded toward a desk near the back. "That's yours. Paperwork comes in the morning; assignments go out by

noon. You make a mistake, someone doesn't eat. Don't screw up."
She nodded and made her way to her seat, ignoring the way the men
continued to glance at her as they worked. The office smelled of ink,
sweat, and something metallic, like old coins. She ran her fingers
over the edge of the desk, taking in the stacks of employment forms,
the dull brass number tokens, the ink-stained logbooks. This was her
job now. This was her new life. And she had no idea what it was
about to bring her.

Chapter 23: From Hell to Hope

The Hooverville stretched out like a forgotten city --- an expanse of
makeshift shacks, tattered canvas tents, and the stench of sweat,
sickness, and desperation. Miles, alone again, drifted among them,
head swimming, ribs pressing against his skin like the bones of a
man already half-buried. Now a habit, Miles tapped, a reassuring
reminder that the poison Max gave him long ago was still there,
recalling Max's words, "Someday, you're going to run up against
someone you can't fight with your fists. Be careful with it, but
remember, it's all about surviving."

He learned quickly. Water first. Men bartered for it in tin cups, a
trickle from a battered pump near the railroad tracks. Others begged
for work in town just to buy a few gulps from the saloons that
charged for the privilege. Miles found a different way --- stealing. In
the early morning, before the Hooverville came alive, he watched a
young boy fill a bucket from a spigot behind a store. The boy turned
away for just a moment. It was enough. Miles swiped the bucket,
gulping down the warm, metallic water before slipping into the
labyrinth of shanties before he could be caught.

Food next. His mule meat had long run out. There was no other food.
Not unless you had something to trade, and Miles had nothing.
Instead, he scoured the rail yard and alleyways for scraps. A
discarded crust of bread. A half-eaten can of beans left behind by
some other unlucky bastard. It wasn't enough. The hunger burned
deeper each day.

He watched men waste away in the Hooverville --- good men, strong men, reduced to skeletons as they waited for a chance at the dam. The job was everything. It was life or death. Miles heard the stories in hushed voices around campfires: He overheard a nearby conversation. "You want work? You show up at the employment office with everybody else. They give everybody a look over and pick who they want. Sometimes they pick by skill, maybe sometimes by strength. Everyone gets a number. Then, you pray yours is called."

The next morning, Miles went. The employment office was little more than a dusty building, its steps lined with men. Hundreds of them. Their clothes hung loose; their eyes sunken. Miles blended in easily. A foreman stood at the doorway, barking orders.

Miles inched forward, shoulder to shoulder with the others. A clerk --- just a boy, maybe sixteen --- stepped out, holding a wooden box. One by one, men reached inside, pulling a scrap of paper with a number scrawled on it. Miles reached in and pulled his fate. 27. He held it tight, as if squeezing the paper might somehow squeeze luck into it. He displayed it as best he could, at least making sure it could be seen. Then he waited. Minutes passed like hours. The sun clawed at his skin. Flies landed on his sweat-streaked face. He swayed but forced himself to stay upright. If he fell, someone else would take his place.

Inside, Becky sat at a desk, a pencil tapping nervously against the wooden surface. She wasn't used to this. A week ago, she'd been at home, helping her mother. Now, she was handing out names to the foreman. It wasn't up to her who got chosen. The numbers were drawn, the list was made, and that was that. But when she glanced out the window, she saw him. Number 27. He stood differently than the others. Not taller or stronger --- if anything, he looked worse. Gaunt. Haunted. But there was something in his eyes, something raw, something real, something that made her fingers tighten around the list. His eyes met hers and they locked.

She glanced at the foreman, then down at the paper in her lap. 42 names today. 42 lucky men. He wasn't one of them. Her heartbeat quickened with a feeling of pity. She knew what it meant to tamper with the list. She would lose this job in an instant. But still... Her pencil hesitated. Then, quickly, when she thought no one was looking, she scribbled down one more number attached to a name. 27. The foreman stepped outside and read the numbers. One by one, men stepped forward. Hope flickered in their hollow eyes.

Down to the last number of the day, the foreman shouted, "27." His eyebrows raised as he thought, '27, could that be right?' But he was too busy to go back and recheck the list. He moved on to other duties that would herd the men to their new work assignments. Miles blinked. Had he misheard? Was it a dream? Men groaned around him. Some swore, some shuffled away. He stumbled forward before anyone could change their mind.

As he moved along with the others, he caught sight of her again --- just for a moment. He didn't know her name, didn't know what she had done for him. But their eyes met again, and something inside him stirred. He'd felt it once before, years ago, staring across the grounds at the La Tourette Hotel at Vanessa Holland. That same flicker of longing, of something just out of reach. He thought to himself, 'This time, I will not lose her.' And then the thought was gone. He was inside now, thrust forward into whatever came next.

Section III

Chapter 24: Burning

Albert sat hunched in his small, soot-streaked shack, a lean-to of scrap wood and corrugated metal set against the blackened hills outside Las Vegas. The scent of burning mesquite and piñon pine clung to his clothes, the acrid residue of his work as a charcoal burner settling into the deep creases of his skin.

The mines outside of Las Vegas needed charcoal; it burned cleaner than wood, and albert was one of the men who worked to process converting it from wood, essential for mining operations. Albert could not care less. He hated the work. But for now, it was all he had. He could not catch on anywhere as a bootlegger. Somehow word got out about his sordid past, killing his partner so he could try to hog the profits for himself, and no one wanted to work with him.

Inside, the single room was sparse --- a cot with a rough wool blanket, a small wooden table scarred from years of careless knife work, and a lantern hanging from a hook, its light barely cutting through the thick gloom. His deformed left hand twitched against his thigh as he stared at the wall, his mind consumed with the vision of Nancy at the Ice House, standing too close to that man. Albert had watched from the distance, his pulse thick in his throat, gripping a wooden post so hard with his good hand that his knuckles had gone white. Nancy had noticed him, just for a second, before he slipped away. He had hoped she wouldn't see. But she did.

For years, he had existed on the edges of her life, drifting in and out like the desert wind. He had loved her since childhood --- not just admired, not just longed for, but loved with a fire that never died. And yet, she had never looked at him the way she had looked at his brother, Robert. Or now, the way she looked at the guy at the Ice House.

The very thought made him curl his fingers into a fist, his damaged left hand unable to fully mirror the gesture. A sneer twisted his lips. It wasn't fair. None of it. The way the world, especially the young girls, had laughed at him, mocked him for the hand he had no choice but to bear. The way the girls in town had whispered behind his back when he was a boy, cruel smiles cutting deeper than any knife ever could. They had seen only the flaw. Not the man. Not his mind.

Not like Nancy had. Nancy had been different. She had been kind. She had been soft-spoken, never turning her gaze away from him like the others did. For a time, that had been enough to sustain him. Until Robert took her. And now, she was slipping further away, smiling for another man, perhaps even letting him kiss her in the cool shadows of the Ice House. Albert's breathing grew heavy, and his mind churned with thoughts he could barely control. He could never hurt Nancy. Never. But the anger inside him needed somewhere to go.

And then, like a black snake uncoiling in his chest, his thoughts turned to Becky. She was the age of those cruel girls long ago, the ones who had laughed, whispered, turned away in disgust. Becky, with her beauty, with her unearned youth and wide, innocent eyes. She was just like them, wasn't she? She had Nancy's kindness, but what did kindness matter in the end? He could never lash out at Nancy. But he seethed at the thought of Becky.

A slow, grim smile crept across his face as he sat in the dim glow of the lantern. He traced the edge of his knife along the wooden tabletop, carving deep, jagged lines into the surface. His mind played with ideas, dark and swirling like the smoke from his charcoal pit. She would pay for the sins of all the girls like her.

Chapter 25: Lurking

Becky settled into her new role at the employment office with a determination to prove herself. Despite the one risk she had taken on her first day --- quietly ensuring 27 was among the chosen workers --- she vowed to be nothing less than exemplary in her work. She arrived early, stayed late when needed, and handled the endless stream of men seeking work with patience and efficiency. She kept meticulous records, sorted through applications, and ensured the right forms were processed properly. The supervisors quickly noticed her reliability, and soon, even the hardened employment officers --- men used to the desperate crowds huddling outside every morning --- acknowledged that she was a valuable addition to the team.

It felt good to have a steady income, to know that she and Nancy would no longer have to scrape by on odd jobs and unpredictable earnings from The Desert Sun. They could afford better meals, more stable housing, and even small comforts like a new dress or a night out at one of the town's modest entertainment spots.

Meanwhile, The Desert Sun circulation was improving. Nancy had made herself untouchable among Las Vegas's power players, holding the mayor's secret like a shield against the more corrupt forces that would have otherwise crushed her fledgling newspaper. Advertisers, once hesitant to associate with an independent paper, began to take notice. For the first time, Nancy could see a future where the paper was more than just a struggling passion project --- it could be a real force in the city.

Charlie remained a frequent presence. At first, their meetings had been casual, a way to unwind from their respective workdays over a cold drink in the back of the Ice House. They had a running joke where she would ask, "Do you have any ice?" But, as the weeks passed, their conversations deepened. He made her laugh, something she hadn't done freely in years. He listened, genuinely interested in her thoughts on the city, on life, on Becky's future. There was no rush between them, no spoken confessions, but it was there, growing. A warmth. A closeness. A comfort Nancy hadn't realized with a man since Robert.

For Becky, life was better than it had ever been. She walked through town with a sense of belonging, a confidence that she had earned her place in this rough and restless city. But then, one afternoon, that feeling shifted. It started as a small prick of unease, a sense that someone's eyes were on her as she made her way down Fremont Street. She slowed her steps, glancing over her shoulder, but the street was its usual bustle --- miners on their way to saloons, shopkeepers sweeping their storefronts, women chatting outside the general store. Nothing out of place. And yet... the feeling didn't go away.

She continued walking, her heart picking up speed. The sun was high, casting long shadows against the buildings. Then, out of the corner of her eye, she saw him. Albert! He was across the street, standing just at the edge of an alleyway. Not moving, just watching. Becky's stomach tightened. She turned quickly, forcing herself to keep walking, to keep her breath even. She didn't want to run.

Running meant fear, and she didn't want to give him that. But the crushing feeling stayed with her all the way home, in fact, it never went away.

Chapter 26: Heaven inside Hell

Miles sat wedged in a sea of smelly men on the back of a flatbed truck, the sun beating down on them as the vehicle rattled over the desert road. Dust churned up around the wheels, filling his nose, coating his skin, clinging to the sweat that rolled down his back. His body ached from weeks of hunger, of sleeping in dirt, of walking with nowhere to go. But for the first time in as long as he could remember, he had something: a job. A real one.

He gripped the edge of the truck bed as they barreled forward, the men around him silent, save for the occasional cough or grunt. Faces hollowed by hardship, eyes wary, hands calloused from labor. These were the ones who made it --- who got picked. The unlucky ones were still back in Vegas, waiting for another number to be called, or giving up entirely, turning to whiskey and despair.

They crested a ridge, and there it was --- Black Canyon, the site of the future dam --- a rugged, chaotic landscape --- an overwhelming mix of natural grandeur and human struggle. It's sheer size mesmerizing, its layered rock walls stretching endlessly into the distance, changing color with the shifting sunlight. Miles wasn't awestruck. He was too damn tired. Tap, tap, on the belt.

The truck skidded to a halt in a swirl of dust, and the foreman, a thick-necked man with a sun-scorched face, barked at them to move. Miles hopped down with the others; legs unsteady. They were herded into a mess hall --- a long, low building that reeked of sweat and coffee. Inside, men lined up, metal trays in hand, handing in their meal tickets, and shuffling forward as cooks slopped food onto their plates.

New hires ate once without a company-issued meal ticket. Miles took his tray, eyes widening. Stew. Bread. Beans. Coffee. His hands shook as he carried it to a bench, half-afraid someone would snatch it away before he could sit down. The first bite burned his mouth, but he didn't care. It was thick, salty, real. He ate with a desperation that made the others glance at him sideways, but no one said a word. They'd all been starving once too.

When the meal was over, they were processed --- names scrawled in ledgers, tools assigned, bunkhouses designated. Miles would be housed with the single men. Miles didn't know he was in a place called Boulder City --- entirely constructed by the behemoth Six Companies business that had the contract to build the dam. Wherever he was, it seemed like a dream. He was handed a bundle of clothes --- denim overalls, thick boots, a rough work shirt. He ran his fingers over the fabric. New. Clean. His.

He was led to a barracks, a long wooden structure with rows of bunks. The air inside was thick with the scent of sweat, dirt, and old wood, but Miles didn't care. He dropped onto the first empty cot, feeling the stiff mattress beneath him. A bed. A goddamn bed.

Someone shouted about showers, and Miles forced himself up, following the line of men to a washhouse. Steam billowed from within. He stripped down and stepped under the scalding water, gasping as the heat bit into his skin. He scrubbed with soap until the grime of months swirled down the drain. The feeling of clean was almost unbearable.

Afterward, he pulled on his new clothes. The fabric was stiff, the boots heavy, but he felt --- whole. Everything he wore was new --- except his treasured belt with its secret contents. That night, he lay in his bunk, staring at the ceiling, thoughts of the girl in the employment office endlessly running through his brain. Outside, the desert wind howled, but in here, the men snored, coughed, muttered in their sleep. He turned onto his side, curling his fingers into the thin blanket. It was harsh. It was dangerous. But to Miles, it was paradise. Tomorrow, the real work would begin.

Chapter 27: Work

Day one on the job site. The morning whistle shrieked through the barracks before the sun had fully risen. Miles jerked awake, momentarily disoriented by the unfamiliar sensation of a mattress beneath him. But reality hit quickly --- he was here, in Boulder City, built specifically to house the project's workers. He had a job to do.

The dormitory bustled as men pulled on their stiff work clothes and laced up their boots. Miles followed their lead, adjusting to the routine. In the mess hall, breakfast was oatmeal, toast, and thick slabs of ham. He ate fast, a survival habit ingrained from riding the rails. By the time he stepped outside, the trucks were already waiting. Dozens of men clambered in, Miles among them, and they were off --- bouncing down the jagged road toward the colossal canyon where the dam would rise.

As they approached, the scale of the operation stole his breath. The canyon walls stretched skyward, impossibly steep. Bridges and scaffolding clung to the rock face like spiderwebs, and a constant roar of machinery filled the air. Men swarmed everywhere --- hauling, drilling, scaling. A foreman, stocky and sunburned, pointed to Miles. "You! Ever done construction?" Miles shook his head. "Then you're a shit shoveler. No skill, no problem. You do what we tell you."

His task was an endless repetition of digging and hauling --- digging and hauling --- and dumping --- then digging and hauling again --- and again. Countless other men did the same. Miles was confused. He'd heard words like "engineering marvel" and other eloquent words to describe this dam. What he saw looked nothing like those fancy words, just a giant pile of dirt and stone --- like it could have been made by giant beavers the size of dinosaurs. But he really had no time to think --- just dig and haul, dig and haul. The air was thick with dust, so fine it coated his tongue and burned his throat. Miles sensed some strange looks from the other men, as if to say, 'skinny kid, how the hell did he get here?' Though the food and the showers quickly revitalized his youthful body, he felt a diminished sense of not belonging. The looks made him feel uncomfortable, unwelcomed.

By midday, the sun was merciless. The canyon walls trapped the heat, turning the site into a furnace. Sweat soaked through Miles's shirt, but he kept moving --- because stopping meant getting fired. He thought his first day would have been more glamourous, more exciting. Is this what every day was going to be like? A disturbing answer floated into his head. Yes.

Chapter 28: Mr. 27

Day two working on the job site would apparently have to wait another day. The team's work crew supervisor was called off on an emergency --- something about mishandled dynamite in the canyon. Miles wasn't even sure what dynamite was, but he was sure grateful for an unexpected day of rest.

The weather was mild compared to most other days. Miles felt a gentler sun seem to breathe energy back into his body. He and the rest of the crew had the day to themselves, lazing around outside the barracks. The other men seemed to keep their distance from Miles, many wondering how this scrawny kid kept up, how he didn't collapse after hauling his first load yesterday.

As the day went on, Miles picked up on various conversations some of the more experienced men were having on their unexpected day off. He learned the big canyon they were working on --- Black Canyon --- had Nevada on one side and Arizona on the other. He learned that yesterday he was working on something called the "lower coffer dam," and that others were working on the "upper coffer dam." He learned that these were only temporary dams, which is why they looked so crude.

Listening some more he figured out why workers would often say things like, "Arizona One" or "Arizona Two," and "Nevada One," or "Nevada Two," names for the tunnels being dug deep inside the canyon walls. The upper coffer dam was being built upstream, designed to block the flow of water from the mighty Colorado from getting into the work site and instead channel it all through four massive diversion tunnels --- two on the Arizona side and two on the

Nevada side --- that would literally run the water through the walls of the canyon and empty it out the other side of the lower coffer dam, designed to prevent water from sliding back into the work side once on the other side of the construction site.

When the tunnels and dams were completed, engineers would open the flood gates and send the mighty Colorado crashing entirely around the work site enabling a dry location within the canyon for concrete pouring to build the actual dam --- still a distant vision for the engineers orchestrating the work.

Miles was glad for the information. Tomorrow might be less torturous if he knew the purpose of the work. As he lay on his back chewing a blade of grass, his mind drifted back to Bayonne --- to the day Max recited the newspaper to him from memory. He remembered not understanding what Max was blathering about, but now it all made sense. Of course it did, Max always knew. Max's words drifted back into his head, "First, they gotta make a dry spot where they build the dam, gonna dig four giant tunnels and make the whole fuckin' river go through 'em and around the spot where they build. And this ain't no regular river. This is the wildest God damn river on earth."

Then came the voice. "Hey, look who it is. Mr. 27." Miles barely turned before a loudmouth who already had a reputation and a nickname --- Big Red --- stepped in front of him. A mountain of a man --- all gut, arms like tree trunks, and a face like beaten leather. He grinned, but it wasn't friendly. "Heard a little birdie got you this job, boy."

Miles wiped sweat from his brow, saying in all honesty, "Don't know what you're talking about." Big Red laughed. "Oh, you don't? That sweet little thing in the hiring office? She picked you out. I was right there when it happened. I saw it with my own eyes. Plucked your sorry hide outta the pile." He spat into the dirt. "You couldn't get in on your own?" Miles didn't know, but now it all made sense. How else could he possibly have been selected? But he was here now and he was not about to give it up. He felt the heat rise in his chest. The other men stopped what they were doing. A show was about to start.

Miles had been bullied before --- visions of Pauley O'Donnell's blinding foot in his nose flashed in his head, followed by glimpses of his humiliating loss in the boxing ring to the nameless freckled boy. Max's words echoed in his head, "Never fight in anger." He took a deep breath and focused. Big Red stepped closer. "Tell me, Mr. 27, did you have to bat your lashes for her?" The laughter was louder this time. Miles exhaled slow. Stay quiet? Take the humiliation? No! Never again. "Bring it boy," Miles said.

Miles took a few steps back, rolled up his sleeves just like Pauley had done. He circled as dramatically as he could, not exactly with Pauley's flair, but with similar effect. Big Red was a bit unnerved by Mile's show of confidence. Nonetheless, the big man flexed. With a memory as though it was yesterday, Miles crouched, as Pauley had done, pretending to tie his shoe.

With no shame in imitating Pauley, Miles discretely picked up a handful of warm desert sand, took a few casual steps forward and launched it Big Red's face. As Big Red raised his hands to his eyes, Miles dropped low, as he'd learned from Pauley --- and drove his legs and shoulders with all his might, driving the giant man backwards. He didn't stop until Red's back hit the barracks wall behind him, smashing the air from his lungs. Having re-lived that scene so many times, Miles knew exactly what to do next. He reached up and grabbed the front of Big Red's shirt and pulled sharply downward, allowing Big Red to fall face first into the hot desert ground.

Almost by instinct, Miles did what Pauley had done to him. He reached down to Big Red's lower back, slid his hands under his belt, and pulled the back of his shirt over the top of his head, binding Big Red's arms in his own clothing. Miles made sure to deliver the kicks exactly where he once received them --- one to the ribs --- and two to the big man's nose. Big Red did not move after that. For a second, everything was still. Then, the men started muttering, shifting their feet, waiting to see what would happen next. Big Red coughed, spit blood into the dirt, and sagged into a heap of stillness.

Miles turned to face the crew. "Anyone else got a problem with how I got here?" His voice was steady, cold. Nobody answered. Nobody met his eyes. The other men quietly went back to whatever they were doing before the showdown. But now --- when they looked at Miles, it wasn't with uncertainty. It was with respect.

Miles now had time to think. Feeling nervous now, after it was all over, he shuddered at what the big man could have done to him. Numb, he stared blankly out across a vast expanse of nothing. A feeling came over him, a feeling without words, one that pulsed through his body and quietly suggested, 'You didn't come this far to make the same mistakes again.'

Chapter 29: Pressing Matters

The Desert Sun had come a long way since Nancy took over. What started as a modest endeavor had transformed into a profitable enterprise, shedding light on the stories that mattered most to the people of Las Vegas. Nancy stood behind the counter of her print shop one afternoon, watching the rhythmic dance of the press as it churned out the latest edition. The steady hum was music to her ears, a testament to the hard work and dedication that had brought her this far. She had even hired her first employee.

Ramon was a Mexican immigrant who initially joined Nancy's shop for odd jobs and handiwork. Over time, Nancy discovered his remarkable aptitude for languages; he spoke four fluently, each learned through his own determination and passion. More than that, Ramon shared her fervor for unearthing and telling the truth. This remarkable man had become a self-made journalist, delving into stories with a keen eye and a relentless pursuit of authenticity. His contributions had become invaluable, enriching the paper's content and broadening its reach. He also had a work ethic like none Nancy had ever seen. He wrote columns, fixed screens and doors, and hauled deliveries all at the same time. Nancy was always amazed.

The larger papers would never hire an untrained Mexican immigrant on their staff. Nancy was grateful for their prejudice.

But all was not perfect. As Nancy observed the day's operations, she noticed the press sputtering, its movements jerky and uneven. A sinking feeling settled in her stomach as she approached, inspecting the machinery. She'd been overlooking it, perhaps even denying it, but now it was clear --- the printing press --- the life blood of her operation --- was on its last legs. Ramon's repairs would only be a temporary fix. Replacing it was the only viable option.

Determined, Nancy set out to find a solution. She learned that the only practical way to acquire a new press was to travel to Los Angeles, select the right one, and arrange for its rail shipment back to Las Vegas. Financially, she was prepared for the expense, but the thought of the journey alone was daunting. Charlie, ever supportive, noticed her apprehension. "I'll go with you," he offered. "Andy can handle things at the Ice House while we're gone." Nancy smiled gratefully. "Thank you, Charlie. I think having you there will make the trip more bearable."

The trip would take some planning. Charlie would need some time to make sure things ran smoothly at the Ice House in his absence. Nancy would likewise need to line things up at the office. They hoped Old Bessie, as they'd come to call the machine, could keep on printing for a month or so. As they discussed the logistics, Nancy realized that leaving the shop in Ramon's capable hands would be the perfect opportunity for him to expand his role. She entrusted him with overseeing the daily operations, confident in his abilities.

Chapter 30: Find Her

Despite the backbreaking work, days on end of eating and sleeping and showering slowly infused life into Miles's resilient body. He felt stronger, rejuvenated. In just his first week on the job he saw several men fall to the punishing work, hauled off for medical attention, likely never to return. One died on the spot before he could be helped. But Miles got stronger every day. He easily outworked every man. Supervisors began to notice.

On Sundays, his only days off, except for the day he fought Big Red, Miles would sleep. Deep and long. A kind of sleep he hadn't experienced for years --- a kind of sleep where he didn't have to keep one eye open to ensure no one would jump him for food or money, or even the clothes on his back.

One Sunday he woke feeling stronger than ever. He wanted to do something, but he didn't know what to do. So, he wandered Boulder City. The streets were quiet, the town nothing more than rows of simple houses and small businesses built for the workers who lived and toiled on the dam project. The Bureau of Reclamation, responsible for its construction, made sure it was a dry town, no need to complicate work with alcohol. Dull was an understatement when describing Boulder City.

As Miles walked through the eerily quiet streets, a voice called out to him from the side. "First day off, huh?" Miles turned to see an older man, likely in his mid-thirties, leaning against a building. He was probably one of the married guys, who lived separately from the single men in houses with their families in this part of the town. His hands were calloused, his clothes stained, but there was an easy smile on his face. "Kinda," Miles replied, wiping his brow with the back of his hand. "First day I didn't want to sleep all day." The man nodded sympathetically. "You look like you've had plenty. Name's Joey," he said, extending a hand. "Miles," Miles said, shaking it.

Feeling obligated to make some conversation, Miles said, "Strange town." Joey chuckled, "A lot different than it used to be. Let me tell you, Boulder City may be strange, but it ain't Ragtown. Back before this town existed, when the dam first started hiring, men poured in --- thousands of us --- looking for work. But there was nowhere to go So we made do." Joey flicked his cigarette into the dust and leaned on the porch railing. "We just called it Ragtown, nothin' but tents and lean-tos, thrown up wherever a man could drive a stake. No streets, no electricity, no sewage. Just filth and misery."

Miles listened, picturing the scene. Joey continued, "The heat could hit a hundred twenty. Water was like gold. We had to haul it from the river, and half the time it was so full of silt it looked like mud. People got sick all the time --- diarrhea, fainting, infections. And the ants? Christ, ants were everywhere. You'd wake up covered in them, crawling in your ears, your nose, your mouth."

Miles grimaced as Joey went on, "And when it rained?" Joey laughed bitterly. "The whole place turned to mud. Your tent would flood, your clothes, your blankets, all soaked through, and the next day the sun would bake it all stiff. Try getting a good night's sleep like that."

The only thing Miles could think to say was, "Guess it's a lot better to be here now." Joey laughed and changed the subject. "So, if you're feeling rested, why aren't you out in Las Vegas with the other single guys?"

Miles blinked; his thoughts momentarily frozen. "Las Vegas?" he repeated, unsure of what Joey meant. "I didn't know we could get there from here." Joey chuckled, "Don't you talk to your bunk mates?" Miles realized the men kept their distance since his run-in with Big Red. "Not really," he answered. Joey explained, "The town makes it easy. They want your money. The company bus gets you there easy enough. Everyone calls it the Saturday Night Special. Takes you right into town. Less than an hour." Miles's eyebrows raised. "A young guy like you could likely use some action," Joey winked. "Ah yes those were the days," he mused. "I've had my fun --- booze, gambling, women --- not necessarily in that order."

Miles stood still for a moment, his brow furrowing as he processed the information. Las Vegas? Of course, he knew it was out there. But he had never thought there was any real way for a dam worker to get there from Boulder City. "The company bus?" Miles asked, his voice tinged with disbelief. "You mean there's a way to get there?" "Yeah," Joey confirmed with a nod. "It's cheap, you can find a motel, and then you've got the whole city at your fingertips for a coupl'a days. Gambling, drinks, the works."

Miles shook his head slightly, still processing. He wasn't interested in any of that. The idea of gambling and losing his hard-earned money was out of the question --- and he never had, and never would, touch a drop of alcohol. Not after he saw the kid on the train with jake leg. Not after he saw what it did to Max.

But that's not why Miles was captivated by the thought. Ever since he got to the dam site, he could not get her out of his head. The way she looked at him, the quiet kindness in her eyes. The girl at the employment office. She had to be somewhere in Las Vegas. Joey noticed Miles's mind seemed somewhere else. "You still with me?" he said. Miles snapped back to attention. "Sure am." Well, you missed it this week, but the bus runs every week." Miles nodded, not really hearing Joey's advice. His focus was already set. "Thanks a lot Joey," Miles managed. He started wandering away. Joey shrugged, 'Strange kid,' he thought to himself. As miles walked alone, he said out loud to no one, "find her."

Chapter 31: Reunion

The next week seemed to stretch on endlessly for Miles: five grueling days before having a chance to get to Las Vegas. The work wasn't easy but he handled it better than anyone else. Each day was just a repeat of the one before --- grueling, back-breaking labor under the blazing sun, with each load of dirt making the lower coffer dam just bit bigger. He got used to the constant aching in his bones, and he had a favorite way of passing the time, caught in an endless but delightful loop of thoughts about the beautiful girl he had glimpsed at the employment office --- the mystery girl who caught his eye, though he didn't yet know her name. He kept thinking, 'find her.'

Even the noise of the mess hall and the clatter of trays and silverware didn't completely snap him out of his thoughts. Miles grabbed some food, unaware of what they were serving, and wandered through the bustling room, his gaze still fixed on nothing in particular, his mind distant. His hand gripped his tray tightly as he weaved between the long wooden tables. His body moved on autopilot, but his thoughts were elsewhere.

Without paying enough attention to the real world around him, he bumped into someone --- hard --- a shoulder colliding with his, a jolt that sent his tray flying from his hands. Food spilled across the floor in a messy heap --- beans, potatoes, bread, and a big slice of meat. 'Damn it,' he thought. There was no way he was going to waste that meal. He didn't have the luxury to be picky, and he wasn't about to let this be the day he went hungry. Ignoring the laughter of the nearby workers, Miles dropped to his knees and began gathering the food back onto his plate, brushing it off as best he could. It wasn't pretty, but it would do. He'd eaten much worse before. He wasn't going to let a little dirt ruin his day. Not today.

As he stood up, dusting his hands off, he looked up --- straight into the face of someone he never thought he'd see again. "Billy!" Miles blurted, his voice catching in his throat. Billy's face broke into a wide grin, as if the universe itself had conspired to bring them back together. For a moment, neither of them could say anything. They just stood there, staring at each other like they had seen a ghost. Then, before Miles knew what was happening, Billy pulled him into a tight embrace. The two men laughed, slapping each other on the back, both grinning like a couple of fools.

"Damn, Miles! I can't believe it," Billy said, pulling back just enough to look him in the eyes. "It's been a long time! And here you are, in the flesh." "I thought you were dead, man," Miles chuckled, wiping a tear from his eye. "After the mule... after all that... hell, I didn't know if I'd ever see you again." Billy laughed, "I'm sure they serve mule meat in Hell." Billy didn't know where to start, "What happened to you that night? Hell, I wound up in jail for a night after we split up."

Miles raised an eyebrow. "Jail? What happened?" Billy shrugged with a grin. "I might have gotten into a little scuffle with some folks in town. They didn't take too kindly to my... enthusiasm. But, hey, I made it here, didn't I?" Miles couldn't help but laugh. Billy's luck was as wild as ever.

"Anyway, you and I both ended up getting hired here. And I got a real job too. Not hauling water or digging ditches," Billy said, his voice laced with humor and just the faintest touch of pride. "I'm a high scaler now --- $1.50 a day instead of $0.50 like most jobs. Not too shabby, huh?"

Miles's eyes widened in surprise. "High scaler?" he repeated, as if he couldn't quite comprehend it. Billy explained, "Who'd a guessed being a lumberjack from Vermont can get you a good job in the desert? They told me all that tree climbin' way up high made me the right guy for swingin' from ropes over the canyon." Billy tried to explain, "We swing down the canyon walls and hammer anything that sticks out to smooth the walls. If that don't work, we use dynamite --- the walls gotta be nice and smooth when they start pourin' concrete, or the damn dam's gonna spring a huge leak." Miles didn't quite understand. His jaw was still dropped since he heard $1.50 a day. Billy continued, "Yeah, I know, I know. I'm basically living the high life now. But look, you should join me. It's a damn good gig. You could be making real money. I can get you in. I can show you the ropes."

Miles, was overwhelmed. First by the enormous amount of Billy's pay, then by absolute terror. His mind flashed back to Bayonne. To Carl Callahan, his words still resonating after all these years, "Listen boy, I don't need another God damn driver, loader, or shit shoveler. I got plenty. What I need is a fuckin' fly-boy who ain't afraid of heights. Got it?" Billy snapped his fingers in front of Miles's face, "Miles you still there?" "Still here," Miles said.

They had to eat quickly and get back to work. They caught up as best they could while eating. "I can't believe you made it," Miles said, shaking his head. "We both had our hands full out there. But you really did it. You're here, and you're working at the top of the world." Billy clapped him on the shoulder. "Hell yeah, man. It's a crazy ride,

but it's worth it. We've both come a long way from that damn mule."
"Yeah," Miles said with a wistful grin. "We sure have."

The two men lingered there for a moment, smiling at the memories they had shared, the hardships they'd endured, and the long road ahead. Then Billy clapped him on the back again, this time more seriously. "I'm in the single men's barracks seven," Billy said, Miles replied, "I'm in number four." "Great to see you, buddy! Let's get together soon. I really think I can get you in as a high scaler." Miles nodded. They shook hands and went back to work, knowing they'd soon meet again.

Alone now, the same fear that gripped him years ago gripped him again. His fear of heights. He shuddered, embarrassed to no one but himself. Then, out of nowhere, that same thought that came into his head after beating up Big Red, "You didn't come this far to make the same mistakes again."

Miles was delighted he reconnected with Billy. And happy for the timing. He needed a break from the seemingly endless wait until the end of the week --- to get back to Las Vegas this Saturday --- to find her.

Chapter 32: Found!

The late afternoon sun cast long shadows over Las Vegas, the desert heat beginning its gradual descent. The city buzzed with its usual energy, but inside the employment office, all was quiet. Becky sat at her desk, the soft scratching of her pen the only sound accompanying the ticking clock on the wall. It was Sunday, a day she typically reserved for church and things other than work, but she'd often come by and catch up on unfinished business in the afternoon. Her commitment to her role had only deepened over time, and she took pride in her reputation as a diligent worker.

As she organized the week's paperwork, a movement outside the window caught her eye. Glancing up, she saw a figure standing hesitantly nearby. Recognition flickered in her mind, but she couldn't place him immediately. The young man seemed to take a deep breath as though gathering his courage for something before bending down to pluck a wilted flower from a nearby patch --- a rare find in the arid landscape. Finally, with a determined stride, he approached the door and knocked gently. Curiosity piqued, Becky rose and opened the door. He stood before her, a hopeful smile on his face, holding out the dwindling bloom.

"Did you miss me?" he asked, his tone light and teasing. Becky blinked, taken aback. There was something familiar about him, a memory tugging at the edges of her consciousness. Then it clicked --- was he was the young man she'd seen weeks ago, the one she'd discreetly assisted in securing a job at the dam? Was this 27? Yes. He looked different now, more confident, certainly bigger and stronger --- and cleaner. But with the same eyes. The traces of uncertainty were now replaced with determination. "You certainly look different," she replied, a hint of amusement in her voice.

Miles had indeed found his way onto the Saturday Night Special. It was worth sleeping a night out under the stars --- he was used to that. And here he was the next day, marveling at his good fortune of finding her so soon. Beyond nervous inside by magnitudes, he tried to chuckle confidently, determined to make a good impression. Extending the pitiful flower toward her once again he said, "I just wanted to thank you for adding me to the hiring list. Without you, I'd never have been hired."

Becky graciously accepted the flower. She was touched. But her expression hardened instantly. "I did no such thing," she said firmly, aware of the need to keep her actions discreet. Miles hoped his clear mistake was not too damaging to his chances. Understanding her position, he nodded, letting the matter drop. "I'm sorry, but in that case, may I simply say hello and introduce myself? I'm Miles Tornero, pleased to make your acquaintance."

Impressed by his gentlemanly demeanor, Becky extended her hand --- and played along with the formality. "Well, Mr. Tornero, I'm pleased to meet you as well. I'm Becky McGuire." Miles asked, "Might you be willing to take a stroll?" Hope was evident in his eyes.

Against her better judgment of walking with a strange man, Becky felt a pull toward this earnest fellow. Something in his gaze spoke of sincerity and warmth. "Why certainly, Mr. Tornero," she agreed, a playful lilt in her voice. Miles crooked his arm, and she took it, the gesture both formal and intimate.

They walked together through random nearby Las Vegas streets, the city alive around them yet feeling like their own private world. Their conversation flowed effortlessly, touching upon their pasts, their dreams even, and the serendipity of their meeting.

As the sky tinged with hues of orange and pink, Becky realized the time. "I really must be going," she said, reluctance in her tone. Miles nodded, but he too seemed unwilling to part. "It was a pleasure to meet you." With mock formal charm seeming to work well so far, Miles kept playing the role. "Might I have the honor of your company another time?" Becky smiled, a genuine warmth in her eyes. "Why certainly, Mr. Tornero. I'd be delighted." Becky broke the pattern of pretense and smiled, "And next time we can drop all this formality." Miles laughed, "Thank goodness!" Both laughed and understood --- let's get real next time.

Becky went north, light on her feet. She had never been wooed before. Ogled yes, but never wooed. She very much liked the feeling.

Miles went south, even lighter on his feet, thrilled even. He laughed to himself --- never in his wildest dreams would he ever be thanking Pauley O'Donnel for anything. But now he's had Pauley to thank twice, once for reminding him how to take down Big Red and now, with the image of Pauley strolling the grounds of the La Tourette with Vanessa Holland still searing his brain, for reminding him of the value of presenting oneself to a lady as a gentleman. He mused inside wondering where Pauley might be today, knowing he'd never know.

Chapter 33: Overcoming

The road back to the dam site stretched long and lonely, but Miles hardly noticed. His thoughts were still lingering in Las Vegas, replaying every moment of his meeting with Becky. The way her eyes had flickered with recognition, the soft tone of her voice as she said his name, the way her fingers had felt as they briefly met his in their introduction, maybe most of all the way she seamlessly played along with their exaggerated formalities --- he held onto it all like a precious keepsake.

But as the company bus rumbled toward the towering canyon walls and the unfinished dam, reality set back in. The fleeting dream of the city faded, replaced by the hard truth of his daily grind. The worksite would be waiting for him in the morning, and he'd be back to digging and hauling, trudging through dust and rock in the sweltering sun for a meager fifty cents a day.

And then there was Billy. Billy, with his easy grin and fearless nature. Billy, who had been dangling from the canyon walls as a high scaler, chipping away at rock hundreds of feet in the air, making three times what Miles did. It had been an offhand remark at the mess hall --- a casual "I think I can get you in" --- but it had taken root in Miles's mind. He hadn't answered then, hadn't been ready to face what it would mean. But now, with the buzz of Becky's voice still in his ears and the weight of his future pressing down on him, the offer felt bigger. Three times the pay. Three times the risk. And one unbearable truth --- Miles Tornero was terrified of heights.

That fear had been with him since he was a kid, since the time he climbed that tree and slipped, caught fortunately by branches at the last second but still feeling that awful lurch in his stomach as the ground yawned open beneath him. It had stayed with him through the years, through the train rides West, through every moment he had to so much as look over the edge of something too high. And yet, here he was, considering a job where he'd spend his days hanging from a rope off the side of a canyon.

But fifty cents a day wasn't enough. Not if he ever wanted something better. Not if he wanted to afford trips back to Las Vegas. Not if he ever hoped to have something more than dust in his pockets. The next morning, as the sun rose over the makeshift town of Boulder City, Miles made up his mind.

He found Billy near the tool shed before the morning shift started. The big Vermonter was hefting a brand-new pickaxe, only the best of equipment given to high scalers, whistling a tune that got lost in the sounds of machinery and men shouting orders. When he spotted Miles, he gave a nod. "You look like a man with somethin' on his mind," Billy said, setting the axe down.

Miles took a deep breath. "That offer you made… about getting me on as a high scaler." He hesitated, then forced the words out before he could back down. "I'm in." Billy grinned. "Atta boy. Knew you had it in ya." Miles let out a nervous laugh. "Not sure I do."

Billy clapped a hand on his shoulder, solid as stone. "Well, you're about to find out." He leaned in, lowering his voice slightly. "I'll talk to my foreman. High scalers are in top demand. When he wants somebody, he gets them." Miles knew also, for better or worse, that his work on his current crew was exemplary; they all knew he was a good worker. Billy continued, "They always need good scalers. But I gotta tell ya' --- there ain't no hand-holdin' up here. You either sink or swim."

Miles swallowed hard but nodded. It wasn't too late to change his mind. He could tell Billy to forget it, to pretend this conversation never happened. But he didn't. Instead, he shook Billy's hand. And with that, his fate was sealed.

Chapter 34: Los Angeles

When Becky came home the house was empty, her head still spinning with delight after meeting Miles. She figured her mom must be at the print shop. She didn't want to be alone so she walked over to The Desert Sun. Becky floated through the door, romance still coursing through her body. Charlie was outside doing something with his truck. Almost alarmed, Nancy noticed something different in Becky right away. "Are you okay, dear?" Becky tried to regain some composure. "Yes mama, of course, why?" "You just seem --- different --- that's all." Becky lied, "No mama, just an ordinary catch-up day at the office."

Nancy shifted focus a major business problem at hand. She stood in the center of the small, sunbaked print shop, arms crossed, surveying the scattered tools of her trade, angry with herself for not taking quicker action. She knew the printing press was on its last legs. She knew she had to go to Los Angels to get a replacement. And yet, here she was, looking at a dead pile of junk in the middle of her office.

Ramon had tried everything to fix it. But all things have an end. And this was the end for Old Bessie. With every day without a working printing press, The Desert Sun would lose more influence, more readers --- so hard fought for over the years. Nancy had always known she was running a fragile operation, but this setback had made it clear --- the paper wouldn't survive without the trip to Los Angeles.

Charlie walked in, wiping the sweat from his forehead with the back of his hand. "We're all set," he said. "Truck's ready, fuel's topped off, and I got a few extra cans just in case." With luck they'd be in Los Angeles first thing Monday morning, ready for the long process of shopping for Old Bessie's replacement.

Nancy nodded, her mind still calculating every risk. The journey was long, dangerous in parts, and Los Angeles itself was no picnic. But it had to be done. "Good," she said, forcing confidence into her voice. She stopped for a moment to remember exactly what Charlie was doing for her. She stepped forward, looked into his eyes, kissed him in a bit more than. a friendly way, and simply said, "Thank You." The way she said it said it all.

Charlie could tell she was nervous. He wasn't thrilled about the trip either, but Nancy needed help. "Everything will be fine," he assured her. "I've traveled much worse roads." Nancy exhaled sharply. "It's not just the roads. It's the time away. The paper can't afford to miss issues." "Ramon can handle things while you're gone," Charlie said. Nancy knew Ramon and his staff would have plenty of fresh content waiting for the press once it arrived. Maybe there would be a delay, but they'd do everything they could to minimize it. Ramon, almost always in the office, looked up from some work he was doing with his staff. "I've got this Miss Nancy."

Charlie, continued to try to reassure Nancy. "And Becky will be fine too, she's grown up now." Becky listened intently. Sad for the office, but inside her heart raced. She'd be alone at home. "I'll be fine mama, don't worry about me." She wasn't sure if she meant it, but her mother needed to hear it.

Charlie picked up a box of office supplies Nancy needed for the trip and carried it outside, where the truck sat loaded and ready for the road. The engine sputtered before roaring to life, and Nancy climbed into the passenger seat, glancing back at the print shop one last time.

As she did, she couldn't help noticing a faint but familiar figure watching her from a distance. Albert? No, it couldn't be. Then the figure disappeared. She thought back to seeing Albert at the Ice House. She assumed then that he hadn't seen her. But this time the figure that had just disappeared seemed to have been looking right at her. She shrugged and thought to herself, 'That couldn't have been Albert. If it was, he surely would have come by to say hello, especially since it's been so long since we've seen each other.' The thought passed. There was work to do.

The sun hung low in the sky as they rumbled out of town, dust swirling in their wake. Ahead of them, the long stretch of desert highway promised uncertainty — but also the hope of keeping The Desert Sun alive.

Chapter 35: Out of Jail

Albert had recently emerged from his jail cell. After what seemed like years of trying, he'd finally gotten another bootlegging job. This one too went bad. The judge had said six months with possible time off for good behavior. Maybe he was good, maybe they just got tired of him --- but either way, he was out and back in the world. He didn't have many options. It was back to charcoal burning for the mines.

He hadn't felt the scorching desert sun quite like this in months. The heat hit him like a wall as he emerged from the charcoal pits, the first week of his return to work now behind him. After his long time in jail, the familiar, grueling rhythm of burning charcoal felt oddly comforting. It was a simple life --- one where employers didn't ask too many questions, especially when all you were doing was burning charcoal. They didn't care much about past mistakes, and they certainly didn't care about his history. They just needed strong bodies, and Albert had that.

The first Sunday off after his long first week of work was a strange thing. He'd been locked up for so long, kept from the world. His twisted thoughts became even more twisted, his resentment for others more successful more intense. And now, after so many months of brooding, he was finally free. The time spent in his cell had been a slow torture, the hours filled with fantasies of getting back to town and doing what he'd always done --- watching Nancy and Becky, waiting for the perfect moment to strike.

This Sunday, Albert sat bored and brooding in his shack. His first instinct was to head straight back to the city, to observe Nancy and Becky from the shadows, to watch their every move. He'd spent months thinking about this moment --- imagining how he'd return to town and take advantage of any opportunity to get alone with Becky.

He wandered to Nancy's print shop. He had no idea what Nancy was up to, but Albert noticed something that piqued his interest. Nancy and the man he saw her with at the Ice House stood next to a truck --- packed with bags and suitcases --- clearly, they were going somewhere. He writhed with jealousy as he watched the man. But his hard heart softened when he saw Nancy. He would always love her and he knew he could never have her. He saw Becky inside the office. She was another story. He always seethed when he saw her. He thought back to how she seemed so revolted by his hand as a child --- his warped mind believing she was like all the other young girls who mocked him in grade school. He needed so much to make Becky pay --- for her transgressions and those of all the other girls. But Nancy and Robert had always been in the way, always getting in between him and Becky. Even with Robert gone now, it was still hard to get close to her when Nancy was always there. But now it looked like something was about to change.

Albert didn't know where they were going, but it didn't matter. He could see the direction they were heading, the truck pulling away from the house. He'd seen enough to know that once they left, Becky would be alone. It was all Albert needed to know.

He felt a pulse of excitement. Nancy would be gone for a while. And Becky? She'd be all alone. He knew exactly what he had to do. He couldn't do anything today, too many others in that office --- not enough time today to savor what he had in mind. He'd wait.

He relished the idea. The thought of Becky, unguarded and vulnerable, sent a shiver down his spine. He could already picture it --- her alone, with no one to stop him. He'd waited too long for this. He'd thought about it endlessly in the dark of his cell. And now, finally, it was within his reach.

Chapter 36: Miss Me?

Becky spent a strange night alone at home Monday night, not thinking about being alone, just thinking of Miles. Tuesday morning an idea popped into her head. He came to visit her. Why can't she go visit him? Her mother's car had been left behind. Nancy didn't tell her not to drive it. Who would know? And if anything went wrong, she'd deal with it later. After all, it wasn't like she was going to be gone long.

She dragged herself through a humdrum day of work at the employment office and, after leaving early feigning a headache, against what she knew her mother would say, found herself driving Nancy's old sedan through Las Vegas and out route 93 on her way to Boulder City. Her heart raced with excitement and nerves in equal measure. The open desert stretched out before her and she could hardly believe she was about to take the wheel, so to speak --- both literally and figuratively.

The desert, while foreign to her, felt oddly familiar in a way. The roads seemed to beckon her toward something she wasn't entirely sure she was ready for. But with the memory of Miles's friendly smile still lingering from their first meeting, she couldn't shake the feeling that something was pulling her toward him.

When she reached the outskirts of Boulder City, the small, modest homes that made up most of the city scape came into view. She parked the car next to a giant boulder near a row of barracks, oddly mixed with the single home structures. Stepping out into the dusty streets, her heart thudded in her chest. The world felt larger here than she had expected. She didn't know where he would be, but she'd find him. She had to.

She wandered, uncertainty gnawing at her as she searched. Boulder City wasn't much more than a few rows of homes and open space; everything about it was temporary, just like the people. She figured he must be somewhere around. After all, a place like this didn't offer much else to do. Her steps slowed as she approached the old stone walls of the barracks. Men passed along the streets, looking tired after a hard day of work, but none were Miles.

It was then that she saw him walking from the mess hall towards the barracks. As he approached, he held a hand to his forehead like a visor --- hoping to get a view of what he was seeing. Could it be? His pace quickened. His heart raced. He ran up to her --- surprised, amazed. In the same tone, the same playful manner he had used when knocking at the door of the employment office to meet her, she smiled and said, "Miss me?"

He'd clearly not expected her to come, much less drive all the way here to find him. "I'm sorry," she said with a playful tilt of her head. "Was I interrupting anything?"

Miles chuckled, shaking his head. "Not at all. What are you doing here?" "I came to see you," she said, a little more boldly than she had planned. "I thought I'd find you, so... here I am." A beat of silence passed between them, filled with the unspoken understanding that this was more than just a casual visit. There was something between them that neither had fully put into words yet. "Well, I'm glad you came." His voice softened, and he stepped toward her. "I'm glad you found me."

She could feel her heart race again, and she tucked a strand of hair behind her ear. "I guess I'm a little... forward." "Not a problem," he said with a grin. "Let's take a walk. You came all this way." As the sun began to set, they walked through the town's boundaries, the dry, still air of the desert surrounding them. Sounds from the town got fainter and fainter and soon they were alone, out beyond the reach of the city limits.

Becky's mind was full of questions she wasn't sure how to ask. She wanted to know more about him, about why he was here, about how he felt --- but the words slipped away, leaving only the hum of her thoughts and the heat of the sun overhead. Instead, she stole glances at him, trying to read his face, unsure of what she saw there. But when she looked at him, she didn't feel nervous or uncertain --- just alive, the air between them charged with something electric and undeniable.

They came to a patch of soft sand, looking for a place to rest, the desert around them stretching in all directions, vast and empty. Miles paused, glancing down at her. "Is this... okay?" he asked politely. Becky felt her pulse quicken. She nodded, her voice barely above a whisper. "It's fine." For a moment, neither spoke. But then, without warning, Miles stepped closer.

The air between them felt thicker now, charged. Becky's breath caught in her throat as he cupped her face gently with his hands, his touch light but warm. "Becky," he said, as though trying to remember her name, trying to hold onto the reality of the moment. And then, he kissed her. It was tender, an exploration of newness and curiosity. His mind flashed back years ago to Hannah's farm. "Slowly, always slowly, like this," he remembered.

It was in this kiss that Becky felt something stir within her. The fear she'd always carried, the uncertainty of intimacy, seemed to evaporate in his arms. For a moment, she was free --- free of the past, free of Albert's putrid memories, free of the world that had taught her to fear closeness. This was different. Miles was different. He drew back slightly, his breath coming in short bursts, his eyes searching hers. "Are you sure?" he asked, voice full of care. "I've never been more sure of anything in my life," Becky whispered, her hands finding the fabric of his shirt.

And there, in the privacy of the desert, surrounded by nothing but the stillness of the land, they made love. It was spontaneous, raw, yet tender. It was more than just an act --- it was a giving of trust, an unspoken promise that neither of them had expected, but both had yearned for. He was grateful for Hannah's lesson --- how to love a woman gently, how to be present, to give her more than his body but his heart, too. Becky had never known such tenderness. Growing up in a city where men ogled and touched women without consent, she had been afraid --- afraid of intimacy, afraid of being vulnerable. But with Miles, it was different. She wasn't afraid anymore. The love that bloomed between them in the open desert was something she would carry with her forever.

As they lay side by side, the vast desert stretched on endlessly before them, the quiet hum of the world almost too much to bear. Miles ran a hand through her hair, and Becky smiled at the simple pleasure of it all. "This... is more than I expected," she said, her voice quiet but full of wonder. He smiled softly. "Me too."

Dark now, they walked silently back to town, back to the car. It was time to leave. Becky looked at Miles and smiled. "My mom is away for a week or two in Los Angeles---just in case you might be around for a visit next Saturday night. I could use the company" Miles smiled back, "I'll be there ten minutes after the bus pulls up."

Chapter 37: Facing Fear

After yesterday, the real world of work would be a hard place for Miles to live in. But the Boulder Dam project was nothing if not demanding. It stopped for no one. And if anyone stopped for it, they'd be cast aside like yesterday's newspaper.

The midday sun beat down on the dam site, the heat shimmering off the canyon walls like waves off a furnace. Miles wiped the sweat from his brow, staring up at the towering rock face where men swung from ropes like spiders, chiseling away at the stone. The high scalers.

It had been a while since Billy made his offer, and Miles had spent every waking hour wrestling with his decision. Fifty cents a day digging and hauling on the coffer dam barely covered his food and bunk. A dollar fifty as a high scaler? That was real money. A man could make plans with that kind of money, real plans. And for the first time in his life, with thoughts of Becky dancing in his mind, he wanted to be able to make plans ---not just for tomorrow --- but for much farther down the road. But the thought of dangling hundreds of feet in the air with nothing but a rope keeping him from certain death? It turned his stomach. It clenched his body with fear.

And yet, here he was at Billy's high scaler work site. Miles was amazed at some of the privilege and power that high scalers had. It was by far the hardest position to fill and Six Companies gave them a lot of leeway. So, when Billy told his supervisor he had a good candidate, it was almost like magic that Miles was given permission to pay Billy a visit. Miles seemed like anything but a good candidate, but no one needed to know. Miles and Billy were close friend, they'd been through thick and thin. Billy had no problem going out on a limb for his buddy. "You sure about this?" Billy asked, standing beside him near the edge of the canyon. "No," Miles admitted. "But I'm doing it anyway."

Billy grinned and clapped him on the back. "That's the spirit." Miles forced himself to take a step forward as a foreman approached. "You the new guy?" the man barked. Miles swallowed hard. "Yes, sir." Billy vouched for him. "Good. No room for cowards up here. You fall; you're done. No second chances." Miles nodded, his throat dry.

The next few hours were a blur. The men fitted him with a rope harness, checked the knots, and handed him a belt full of tools and a pouch of dynamite. He tried to ignore the way his hands trembled as they led him to the edge. Billy went first, swinging out over the abyss like it was nothing. "See?" he shouted. "Piece of cake!" Miles didn't move. "Come on!" Billy called. "Ain't no way to do it but to do it."

Frozen by fear, Miles's mind took him back in time. He saw Carl Callahan's cruel face in front of him, shouting "Get the fuck outta here, I got work to do." The words seared his memory, filled him with rage. He never wanted to be humiliated like that or miss an opportunity like that ever again. With a deep breath, Miles forced himself over the ledge. The moment his feet left solid ground; his stomach twisted. The canyon floor stretched out below, impossibly far away. His breath came in quick, panicked gasps. His fingers clenched the rope so tightly they burned.

Then as he swung out over the canyon, his stomach turned again --- this time for an entirely different reason. Before he could stop himself, he vomited. The mess scattered in the wind, vanishing into the void below. He clung to the rope, panting, embarrassed. Laughter erupted from above. "Welcome to the high scalers!" someone called.

Billy, still swinging nearby, gave him a thumbs-up. "Happens to all of us, pal. Now get to work!" Miles's hands were still shaking, but he forced them to move. Swinging gently, he reached out and slammed a sledgehammer against the rock. The vibration shot up his arm, but the stone cracked. Again. And again.

Time blurred. The wind howled through the canyon, dust choked the air, and the sun beat down mercilessly, but Miles worked. He swung and he chipped. Billy called, "Time for dynamite, you can do it!" Emboldened, Miles recalled what Billy taught him. He struck the match and lit the fuse. The wick hissed. "Go, go, go!" Billy yelled. Miles swung away just as the explosion rocked the canyon. A thunderous boom echoed through the dam site, dust and debris flying in every direction. Miles let out a wild, unrestrained Yahoo! as he sailed through the air. From above, Billy laughed and did the same.

Miles landed against the rock face, breathless, heart pounding. His body was exhausted, his hands raw, but he was grinning.

He had done it. He didn't have to return to the coffer dam. Miles was a high scaler now.

Chapter 38: Finally, Saturday

Becky counted the days, delighted her mother was away, delighted she was bold enough to invite Miles to her home in her mother's absence. Was it only yesterday she made love for the first time? It seemed like forever. Does she still have to wait two more days to see him again? She didn't know if she could wait that long. She busied herself shuffling useless papers at the office. Luckily, she now knew her job inside and out. No one notice how little she was paying attention.

Finally, Saturday arrived. The morning dragged endlessly. The afternoon even longer. But now it was evening. Becky wore her nicest dress. She made a fresh stew. She hoped Miles would like it. And then, she waited.

As if she thought it would never happen, there was a surprising knock on the door. Her heart leaped. He was early! Becky ran to the door. She knew what she was going to say, "miss me?" She swung the door open to greet him, and that's when her heart stopped.

It was Albert. His hulking form filled the doorway, and his twisted grin made her blood run cold. He wasn't supposed to be here. She hadn't invited him. But Albert had a way of showing up when she least expected it. He had seen Nancy leave. He knew she'd be alone. "Hello, Uncle Albert," she managed, bathed in fear, but hopefully appearing pleased and surprised.

He walked in uninvited, as if it were a friendly visit. Becky was too shocked to speak any more. She knew the truth. She had seen that look in his eyes too many times before. Albert was here with a purpose, and it wasn't to catch up on old times.

Becky stiffened, trying to hold it together, but the tremble in her hands betrayed her. She feared that one slight indication of fear or knowing would trigger him to pounce. Albert gently placed his left arm around her, his deformed hand like an anvil on her shoulder. He guided her to the kitchen, Becky too paralyzed by fear to resist.

He stood by the kitchen table. feigning casual conversation, waiting for his moment to strike. "How have you been, sweetheart?" Becky could feel it --- the same sense of dread that had haunted her as a child when Albert would visit her family farm in Lincoln. She had been afraid then, and now, years later, that fear had only grown stronger. After lifetime of repressed memories, locked with the vicious determination of a child desperate to survive, the visions overcame the barriers and came crashing through, visions from the farmhouse, memories now as clear as day --- of Albert's clawed left hand pushing up hard between her legs.

Chapter 39: A New Scarf

The bus rumbled forward towards Las Vegas. By now, Miles was used to the Saturday Night Special ride into town. But this was no ordinary Saturday night --- indeed it was "special." He couldn't wait any longer to finally see Becky. It had been a long almost endless week. He struggled every day. At times he had to force her out of his mind. His life depended on it. His work was now full with dangerous high scaler duties. He had no choice but to focus on life or death. Still visions of Becky barged their way into his head. As the bus bumped along, he couldn't wait to share the news with her about becoming a high scaler.

Every day these few days away from her was spent on the narrow ledges of Black Canyon, his body suspended hundreds of feet above the river basin below. His fingers gripped the ropes, the leather gloves he'd been issued already wearing thin. He heard drills hammering into the rock somewhere above him, and dynamite blasting nearby, but sometimes the sounds barely registered. Two things constantly clashed for attention in his mind --- the sheer, brutal task of surviving the work of a high scaler and the thought of Becky waiting for him back in Las Vegas.

Miles had a hard but thrilling week as a high scaler. By Saturday, his body was aching, his arms felt like lead, but he knew he belonged up there. He conquered something that had broken him before. And yet, as much as he wanted to bask in that accomplishment, he found his mind constantly drifting back to Becky. And he couldn't wait to tell her all about it.

He had a scarf on his lap. Soft, delicate, deep red like the desert at sunset. It cost more than a week's pay from his old job. But he didn't care. He could afford it now. He hoped she would love it. As he moved along, the bus seemed to move slower and slower. One more hour and she'd be in his arms again.

Chapter 40: A saving knock

Becky stood frozen in the kitchen in front of Albert. Small talk wandered from charcoal burning to Nancy going to buy a new printing press. But talk seemed to be running out. And then what? Suddenly, the sound of a knock at the door broke through her terror.

Miles? Becky felt her breath catch in her throat. Albert's demeanor immediately shifted --- he was startled, rattled. Becky said, "Excuse me, I think it's a neighbor" as casually as she could, hoping Albert would allow her to answer the door. He did, and Becky walked at what she hoped looked like a normal pace to the door as Albert cautiously watched.

As Becky opened the door, Miles knew something was not right. He saw a hulking figure of a man in the kitchen. Albert's hand clenched as he composed himself, gathering up his famous false charm from within. Albert approached the doorway. Becky, noticing the scarf in Miles's hand, made a fake introduction. "Uncle Albert, this is Frank Handy our neighbor." Miles played along sensing something in the air. "Um --- Nice to meet you. Yes, I, ah, just stopped by to drop off this scarf my mom borrowed from Nancy," hoping to sound believable. Becky thought quickly, "Please come in Frank, maybe you'd like some lemonade?" Albert panicked inside. He didn't want anyone to know him, not with what he had in mind. He said politely, "Nice meeting you Frank, I really must go. Becky, I'll see you soon." He glared at her out of sight from Miles.

The minute Albert left, Miles tried to ask what just happened. But before he could Becky ran straight into his arms. She buried her face against his chest, trembling uncontrollably now, the weight of the fear she had carried for so long finally crashing down on her. "Miles, it's him. Albert... he's back. I --- I don't know how to stop him." Her voice broke with the words, and she felt a sense of shame rise within her. She hadn't told anyone. Not until now. Not until Miles.

Miles held her tightly, trying to make sense of what she was saying. He hadn't known Albert's name. He hadn't known who the giant man in the house was until now. But the way Becky clung to him, the desperation in her voice --- it was clear this wasn't just some casual encounter. There was a history here. A history that was dark and painful. Becky pulled back slightly, looking up at him with wide, fearful eyes. "He's going to come back. He's just waiting for you to leave. I know it. He always does this. He's waiting for the right moment."

Gradually Becky told Miles the story. Not everything, but everything he needed to know. Miles's body filled with rage. He wanted to tear this "Uncle Albert" apart. But the image of the beast of a man was clear. Miles's knew that even with his street-smart fighting skills he'd never defeat Albert. Becky shivered, "He's never going to stop. He's coming back. I know it." Miles sat, dejected, unable to figure out a way to help.

He took a deep breath. He thought about seeking help, reporting his behavior. But Albert had done nothing yet except visit his niece --- and in a town like Las Vegas, a vague accusation would mean nothing. He thought about the two of them fleeing the house --- but sensed that would be only temporary. Something had to be done soon. He tapped his belt, now a habit. And then, of course --- the poison! Max's words raced through his head as though he said them only yesterday, "Someday, you're going to run up against someone you can't fight with your fists. Be careful with it, but remember, it's all about surviving."

Miles wasted no time. "I have an idea. I've got a way to stop him. But --- it's dangerous. I need you to trust me." Becky looked at him, confused but willing to listen. "What do you mean? What are you talking about?" Miles hesitated, his hands trembling as he reached for his belt. From the hidden slit cut years ago, he pulled the small foil packet. He handed it to her. "Poison" he whispered, the gravity of his words sinking in. "It's been with me for years. I've kept it, always thinking one day I would need it. But never like this." Becky studied the packet. She had heard of poison used in the world of spies and criminals, but she never thought she'd see it used for something like this.

"How does it work?" she asked, already knowing the answer, but needing to be sure. Miles explained, his voice quiet but resolute. "It's arsenic. It works slowly, but it works. You can put it in something he'll eat. Becky thought out loud, "He's always been ravenous, he eats like a wild animal." Miles answered, "Then you just need to make sure he eats it all, and then we wait. Thirty minutes. That's all it takes."

Miles absorbed the plan. This wasn't what he had expected when Max gave him the packet as he lay dying in Bayonne. But he understood the danger Becky was in --- and it seemed the only way to keep her safe. "Okay. What do you need me to do?" he asked, his voice tight with resolve.

Becky formulated the rest of the plan. She had the stew in the ice box --- Albert's favorite. He'd never turn it down, especially not when he was hungry, and Becky knew he'd devour it without hesitation. "He's outside this house right now. I know it. I'll pretend like everything's normal," she said. "I'll act like I don't know what's coming. But I'll get him to eat every bite. Then, we wait and hope it works."

They spent a few minutes going over the details, making sure everything was set in motion. Miles agreed to leave through the front door, making it obvious that he was leaving. That way, Albert would think it was safe to return. "I'll say goodbye loud enough for him to hear me," Miles said. "That should be enough to get him back in here." I'll wait outside and watch."

Becky knew Albert would be lurking, waiting for the moment when Frank left. It was a calculated risk, but they didn't have many options. The time came to act. Miles stepped outside and said as loudly as he could without yelling, "Good night, Becky. Please thank your mom for the use of that lovely scarf." Becky answered, "Oh for sure, Frank, and please say hello to Mary from both of us." "Thank you for the lemonade." "You're very welcome, good night." With that their fates were sealed. Becky went back inside. Miles circled around to the rear of the house.

As the minutes passed, the tension in the house grew unbearable. Becky began preparing the stew, her hands steady despite the storm brewing in her chest. She set the table, tried to keep her mind off the coming confrontation.

When Albert finally returned, he seemed relaxed, almost casual, a distinct smell of liquor on his breath. He didn't suspect a thing. "Hello again, Becky," he said. "I didn't want to intrude on your neighbor's visit." "Oh, that's ok Uncle Albert," Becky said, somehow steadier knowing Miles was nearby. "I'm glad you came back." She smiled at him, trying to make her voice sound normal. "I made your favorite, Uncle Albert. Stew. I thought you might like some."

He nodded eagerly, his twisted grin spreading across his face. "You know me too well," he said, taking a seat at the table. "I'm starving." Becky held her breath, watching him shovel the poisoned stew into his mouth. She fought the urge to look at the clock --- fought the urge to rush things. The minutes passed like hours, but she kept her cool, tried to keep the conversation going, to stall for time. Albert, oblivious to the poison, ate with ravenous hunger, his eyes gleaming as he enjoyed the meal. Stew covered his chin and slithered in his bushy mustache. Becky silently prayed.

Thirty minutes. Albert kept eating. After a third helping, Becky could get him to eat no more. He put down the spoon, wiped his mouth, and took out a flask from his pocket. He unscrewed it and began drinking, his movements becoming more erratic. He started looking at Becky with that familiar, unsettling gaze. His eyes flickered with something dark and predatory.

Forty minutes. Becky swallowed; her throat dry. She tried to make conversation, but Albert was growing impatient, moving closer, his eyes fixed on her. Then, he stood up. "I've been waiting a long time for this, Becky," he said, his voice thick with menace. "You're just like all those other girls who made fun of me." He grabbed her roughly, holding her with his grotesquely deformed left hand. His other hand reached for her, pressing her against him, his breath rancid with whiskey.

Becky froze, fear crashing through her like a tidal wave. Miles watched in horror from outside --- 45 minutes and not a hint of effect from the poison. And in that moment, a crash --- Miles. He had seen enough. He could wait no longer. Miles burst through the door, desperate to stop Albert. He lunged at the larger man, fists flying, but Albert was like a mountain. With terrifying ease, he grabbed Miles and tossed him aside like a ragdoll, slamming him into the furniture with a sickening crunch.

Albert turned his attention back to Becky, and Miles slowly got to his feet, gasping for air. He tried to charge again, but Albert caught him with one hand, lifting him off the ground, choking the life out of him with a grip that could crush stone. Becky's heart raced as she watched Miles go limp, his eyes rolling back into his head.

But then something changed. Albert's face began to twist. His chest heaved. His breath became ragged. He staggered, clutching his throat, his knees buckling. The poison was working. Albert's face contorted in agony as his body began to convulse. He dropped to the ground with a sickening thud, his last breath escaping in a wheeze.

Becky watched in stunned silence as Albert's life ebbed away. The man who had haunted her for so long was finally gone. Miles, still gasping for breath, crawled over to her. Together, they sat in the silence that followed, knowing the nightmare was over.

Chapter 41: No Questions

Hours passed like days. Albert's silent mass in his final heap turned cold and stiff --- but somehow still felt dangerous.

Miles and Becky stared --- away from him when possible --- barely moving --- barely able to form words, let alone a plan. Finally, Becky spoke, "Wait here. I'll be back in an hour." Miles didn't question. They embraced. She left.

As Miles thought he had reached his breaking point for sitting alone with a corpse, clatter and purpose marched through the front door.

Becky led, followed by Ramon, followed by four of Ramon's relatives --- strapping young men each with shovel in hand --- none with questions.

When Nancy was planning her journey to Los Angeles and putting faith in Ramon to handle things in her absence, she had no idea just how capable he'd be of proving that she had made a powerfully good decision.

Chapter 42: The Truth Unburied

Nancy sat stiffly in the worn chair by the window, her fingers curling and uncurling in her lap. Her suitcase sat unpacked next to her. The dust of the road still clung to her travel clothes, and a faint smudge of ink streaked across one sleeve --- a reminder of the printing press she had been so excited to send home.

Now, that excitement was gone, drained from her like the last drops of water from a cracked canteen. She stared at Becky, her eyes clouded with disbelief. "Albert is dead?" The words barely left her lips, as if saying them would make them more real. Becky stood across the room, hands trembling at her sides. "Yes, Mama." Nancy's expression barely changed.

She was still absorbing the shock when her gaze sharpened, flicking over Becky with something colder, something angrier. "And who is Miles?" Her voice was sharp, laced with judgment. "You're spending time with a whoring, drinking dam worker?" Becky flinched, but she had expected this. "Mama, please… " Nancy shook her head, her mouth twisting in disgust. "I was gone a week, Becky. A week! And I come back to this?"

"My dear Albert dead? And you, tangled up with…" Charlie shifted uncomfortably beside her, his gaze darting between the two women. Becky caught his hesitation and seized it. "Charlie, could you give us a moment?" Nancy turned sharply toward him, as if just realizing he was there. "No. He stays." Becky's voice softened, but there was steel beneath it. "Mama, please." Charlie hesitated, then exhaled and stood.

"I'll be outside." He shot Nancy a brief look before stepping onto the front porch, closing the door behind him.

Silence stretched between them, heavy as lead. Nancy's fingers clenched into fists. "I don't understand," she murmured. "Albert was a good man. He loved us." Her voice cracked on the last words. "No, Mama," Becky whispered. "He didn't." Nancy's head snapped up, her brow furrowing in confusion. "What are you talking about?" Becky swallowed hard, her mouth dry. Her whole body was trembling now, but she forced herself to speak. "Uncle Albert --- he hurt me. When I was little. He came into my room at night. He…" She choked on the words. "He was not a good man, Mama." Nancy paled. "No," she said immediately, shaking her head as if the very idea was impossible. "No, Becky. That's not true."

Becky's eyes filled with tears, but she didn't look away. "It is true." Nancy's breathing grew ragged. "I --- I never saw anything. He was always so kind, so loving." "Mama," Becky said softly, stepping closer. "He was careful. He made sure you didn't see." Nancy's hands went to her mouth, her whole body shaking, her denial struggling to survive. "No… no… I would have known. I would have…" Becky knelt beside her mother, taking her hands in hers. "You couldn't have known. He made sure of that." Nancy squeezed her eyes shut, her breath coming in shallow gasps. Nancy stood, pacing the small room, her movements erratic. "And Miles? He killed Albert?" Becky nodded. "He saved me, Mama. Albert came after me, and Miles stopped him.

Nancy turned away, gripping the edge of the table like it was the only thing keeping her upright. When she finally spoke, her voice was hollow. "And you love him?" Becky hesitated for just a moment before answering. "Yes." Nancy turned slowly, her eyes searching Becky's face. "He's not like the others?" Becky shook her head. "No. He's strong, but gentle. He's seen hard times, but he doesn't let it make him cruel. And Mama… " She took a deep breath. "He understands. About Albert. He understands pain."

Nancy stared at her daughter for a long moment, her expression unreadable. Then, finally, her shoulders slumped, as if the weight of everything had finally settled upon her. "I was blind," she whispered. "All these years. I let a monster near my child." She repeated slowly, painfully, "All. These. Years." Each word dropped hard like a boulder crashing through thick ice. Becky reached for her, her voice firm. "Albert did that. Not you." Nancy gasped with sickening realization, "The Ice House --- and the print shop --- how could I be so..." She let out a trembling breath, her hands still shaking. "I'm so sorry," she murmured, "I am so sorry!"

After a long, silent, sobbing hug, Nancy locked eyes with her daughter. "I want to meet him." Relief flooded Becky, but it was tinged with something else --- something heavy and uncertain. The truth was out, but the road ahead was unclear. Still, for the first time in her life, she felt safe.

Chapter 43: A New Impression

The harsh desert life in Las Vegas had a way of forcing people forward, no matter how dark the past, no matter how difficult the road ahead. Albert was dead, buried deep in the desert sands where no one would ever find him. No one looked for men like Albert. He was a shadow in the world, someone who barely existed in the first place. And now, he was gone. Life had to move on.

The printing press finally arrived on Friday, a massive machine that dominated the small workspace with its heavy steel frame and intricate mechanisms. It came with a stack of instructions, each more complicated than the last. Ramon had called in several of his workers to help with the setup, and even then, the process was slow and frustrating.

The excitement of having the press was tempered by the sheer amount of work ahead. By the time Saturday rolled around, Miles arrived in town on the bus --- the Saturday Night Special --- but this time, he wasn't just here for Becky. He was here to meet Nancy. Becky had told him Nancy wanted to meet him, and Miles, understanding the weight of that, wanted to make a good impression.

They spoke as briefly as possible about the Albert calamity. There seemed nothing more to say, a terrible way to get to know each other. But, when he found out about the press, he didn't hesitate --- a chance to change the subject, a chance to move on. "I can help with that," he said, rolling up his sleeves. Nancy watched as he jumped right in, working alongside Ramon's men without hesitation. He wasn't just offering to help --- he was actually useful. He handled the heavy parts, read through the instructions carefully, and asked smart questions about how the press was supposed to function.

Charlie took a liking to Miles almost immediately. Nancy had been cautious --- curious about the man who had suddenly become so important in Becky's life --- but seeing Miles work alongside them, patient, steady, and capable, put her at ease. He wasn't just some dam worker looking for a good time in Vegas. He was different. By the time the press was fully assembled, the sun had begun to set, casting long shadows over the small shop. Everyone was exhausted but satisfied.

That evening, Nancy, Charlie, Becky, and Miles had dinner together. The conversation was easy, flowing naturally between stories of Las Vegas, the dam, and the future of the paper. Miles didn't try to impress anyone --- he just was himself. Nancy liked that. She watched him carefully, noting the way he spoke, the way he looked at Becky, the way he listened more than he talked. She had worried at first, but now she was beginning to understand. Becky had found someone real.

When Sunday afternoon came, it was time for Miles to catch the bus back to the dam. As always, Becky walked with him to the stop. "Well, what do you think?" she asked. Miles smirked. "I think your mom's got her eye on me. I'm not sure if I passed or failed." Becky smiled. "You passed." Miles pulled her close for a brief moment. "Good." And with that, he boarded the Saturday Night Special once again, heading back to the grind of dam work, leaving behind the city, Becky, and maybe --- toward a new beginning.

Chapter 44: A New Rhythm

As weeks turned into months since Albert's demise, Miles, Becky, Nancy, Charlie, and Ramon fell into a peaceful quiet rhythm, blocking out a black chapter in their lives no one wanted to revisit. High scaling fit Miles to a tee. He and Billy were a team again. The printing press was humming at full steam. Ramon was now a central figure at The Desert Sun. Becky almost ran the day-to-day work at the employment office and was now the lead secretary. If there was anything to be concerned about it may have been with Charlie, who was beginning to read the writing on the wall regarding his business. The dam, when finished would generate so much electricity, there would be no need for an Ice House. Heck, every house in the city would likely soon have refrigerators and freezers. But Charlie wasn't worried. He built that business in no time and was sure he could find something else.

Nancy loved Charlie's quiet confidence. By now she loved everything about him. Occasionally Miles and Becky, especially after stealing a moment of intimacy, would laugh and speculate how Nancy and Charlie did it. They were always so proper, one might never know.

His Saturday nights in Las Vegas became a pleasant routine --- not just to see Becky, but for the quiet dinners with Nancy and Charlie, the easy conversation, the warmth of belonging --- to a family he never had. It felt like a life waiting for him, just beyond his reach. Tonight was no different. A simple evening filled with laughter, shared stories, and lingering glances between him and Becky that said more than words ever could. They took their usual after dinner walk where they'd share a secret kiss --- or more if there was time, and somewhere private.

And every Saturday night included a stay at The Meadows, a spacious but cheap flea bag hotel on the edge of town. Nancy may have liked Miles --- a lot --- but there was decorum. Miles staying with them was out of the question. By now Miles could afford a nicer hotel, but he wouldn't think of it. Staying here meant a lot to him. It reminded him of how he could barely afford it at first, he loved its charm, its familiarity. But mostly he stayed at The Meadows because of Peachy the bright-eyed cheery matriarch of the run-down establishment.

For Miles, no stay at The Meadows was ever complete without a friendly chat with Peachy, usually after coming home for the night after his visit at Nancy's house. It had become a regular routine for Miles. And anyone who knew Peachy knew that any chat with Peachy was a long chat with Peachy. Miles never minded. Peachy lived in Las Vegas all her life. Knew the area, taught him the history. But she also had a way of making all of it personal, and real. He learned to look forward to seeing her on his weekly visits almost as much as he did seeing Becky and Nancy and Charlie.

On a typical ride back to the dam one Sunday, Miles felt relaxed, confident, even happy. But a feeling came about him that took off some of the shine. It asked, 'how long will this last?'

Chapter 45: The Divide

The midday sun on Monday morning hung low over the Black Canyon, casting jagged shadows over the men clinging to the sheer rock face. The wind carried the smell of dust and sweat, and the distant clang of steel on stone echoed off the canyon walls. Miles adjusted his harness and looked down, his stomach tightening. He looked over at Billy, expecting to see his usual confident smiling face --- but something in his friend's face made him uneasy. He seemed sad --- but something more. He wasn't just sad. He was angry.

Billy's calloused fingers curled into fists at his sides as he glared at the dry river basin far below. "Shiny Joe's dead," he said, voice harsh and flat.

Miles stiffened. "What?" Billy turned to him, eyes dark. "CO_2 poisoning. Nevada Two tunnel. Damn compressor failed, and they sent Joe and some others in anyway." He shook his head, his breath coming fast. "They knew, Miles. Six Companies knew that damn thing wasn't working right. But they figured a few dead men were cheaper than fixing it."

Miles swallowed hard down a tightening throat. Shiny Joe. Always laughing, always quick with a story. Gone. Just like that.

Billy's jaw clenched. "And you know what they'll say? Pneumonia. Just like all the others. Forty-two men dead from "pneumonia," and not a single case in town. They're covering their asses, Miles. Hiding the truth so they don't have to pay."

Miles looked away, unable to meet Billy's gaze. He had heard the rumors, of course. Everyone had. But hearing it now, so raw and real, made his chest ache.

Billy's eyes flashed with anger. "But you know what does make the papers? That damn high scaler rescue --- all over the news last year. Sure, it was a hell of a thing, but it's all part of their game. Show the world the heroics, the feel-good stories, and bury the bodies of men like Joe under lies."

Miles knew where this was going. He had heard whispers before --- men talking in hushed voices about unions, about standing up to Six Companies. But he had also seen how that ended --- Billy was not the first seeking fairness.

"Billy," he started, but Billy was already shaking his head. "I'm gonna do something, Miles. I'm not just gonna stand here and let 'em kill people off one by one. I'm going to organize a union fight. Someone has to be brave enough to do it!"

Miles exhaled sharply. "You remember last year? When they shut down that strike? Pinkertons cracked skulls, Billy. Men disappeared. Six Companies runs this job like a damn kingdom. You try to unionize; you'll be out on your ass. If you're lucky."

Billy's nostrils flared. "And if we don't? How many more men gotta die before you decide it's worth it?" Miles looked down at the dust coating his boots. He hated himself for what he was about to say. "I can't do it, Billy."

Billy stared at him, waiting. Miles met his gaze, forcing himself to hold it. "For the first time in my life, I got steady work. Three squares a day. A roof over my head. And I --- I have Becky." He hesitated, then pushed on. "She makes me think about the future. A real one. Not just surviving day to day, wondering if I'm gonna wake up with a pickaxe in my skull or if some company man's gonna decide I ain't worth the trouble."

Billy scoffed, a bitter sound. "So that's it? You're just gonna look the other way?"

Miles took a step closer. "This isn't our fight."

Billy's eyes burned. "It is. It always has been."

Silence stretched between them, thick and suffocating. Miles licked his dry lips. "You're my brother, Billy. You got me this job. And I'd follow you anywhere. But not this. I can't."

Billy's shoulders slumped for the first time, the fight draining out of him. He stared at Miles like he was looking at a stranger. "Maybe I was wrong about you," he said quietly. Miles flinched. Billy turned and walked away without another word.

Miles let out a shaky breath and looked out over the canyon, where the river once snaked below, now blocked by the upper coffer dam. His mind drifted back to a day long ago, standing beside Max as they watched Nicky, the scrappy street dog, square off against the big black German shepherd. Max knew who would ultimately win, even though Nicky ran away. Max's voice echoed in his head. "He knew he had the bad ground, had no way to win, but he'll wait till the fight is on his terms... It's all about surviving." And, for the first time in his life, Miles felt sad about Max being right again.

Chapter 46: The Hollow Canyon

For the next three days Miles avoided Billy. He worked as far away from him as possible. His heart ached. If there was ever a time in his life he might want to drink liquor it could be now --- he wanted to numb this pain. He could not bear to face Billy. He feared their relationship was over. He'd heard already Billy was moving forward without him, recruiting malcontents into action. He admired his friend's courage, but he feared for his friend's life.

On the fourth day, something seemed different. The usual banter of the crew was there, but it felt --- forced --- as if everyone was talking just loud enough to cover up something they didn't want to think about. Billy wasn't front and center as usual. Then his heart sunk. He knew it before he asked, but the words slipped out anyway. "Where's Billy?"

The foreman barely looked up, his face unreadable beneath the brim of his dust-covered hat. His voice was flat, but there was something in it --- something cold, something final. "He's not here."

That was all. Not sick, not moved to another crew, not quit. Just not here. And the way he said it --- the way his eyes dared Miles to ask more --- made it clear that was all he'd ever get. Miles felt his stomach twist violently, but he kept his face still. He swallowed back the bile rising in his throat, forced his shoulders not to tense. He nodded once, a small, indifferent shrug. "Alright."

He turned away before the foreman could see the truth in his eyes. Before anyone could see. Because if they did --- if they caught even a glimpse of what he was really thinking --- he'd be next.

The morning dragged. Miles climbed the ropes with a dull, detached rhythm, hammering away at the rock like a man going through the motions. But his mind wasn't on the stone in front of him. It was on Billy. On what might have happened in the dark of night, behind some alleyway in Boulder City or on the long, empty road to Vegas.

They'd come for Billy. And they'd made sure no one would ask where he'd gone. He let himself slip --- just a little --- letting his boots shift wrong against the canyon face. His hands weren't gripping the rope as tightly as they should have. For the first time since taking this job, he wasn't thinking enough about surviving.

"Watch it, Miles!" someone shouted from above. He blinked, realizing he'd leaned too far out over the edge. His heart should have kicked in, his pulse should have spiked. Instead, he just pulled himself back lazily, as if he didn't care either way.

Maybe he didn't. Because something wasn't right anymore. The canyon itself felt different, like it had lost something --- like the walls had closed in just a little tighter, and the sky had stretched a little farther away. Something had changed. And something needed to change. He thought about Billy's words --- "How many more men gotta die before you decide it's worth it?"

Miles thought he'd made the right choice. He had told himself that keeping his head down, doing the job, was the smart move. But now, hanging from a rope over the abyss, he wasn't so sure.

Chapter 47: The Floodgates of Change

For Miles, working without Billy was like swinging his glimmering pickaxe without a handle. Empty. Useless. But there was more to Billy's loss. The whole canyon seemed to be changing --- shifting. Conversations were different --- more vague --- more talk about "next steps," and concrete. Today that sense of change was more real, more alive. As the sun continued climbing above the jagged ridges of Black Canyon, a buzz started moving through camp like static on a wire. Word spread --- not official, but enough to stir the men --- that this was the day. The day they would open the gates and channel the mighty Colorado through the diversion tunnels.

Miles had heard it from a guy on Tunnel Two, a gopher who'd been hauling cables since the first blast back in '31. He said the engineers had finally given the green light. The last barriers on the upper coffer dam were ready to drop. The tunnels --- all four of them --- were clear and waiting. The river was going to be turned.

For months, maybe years, all this endless work all felt like a fool's errand to many of the workers, each doing their own tiny part of the grand scheme. Endless blasting and digging, carving out monstrous holes in the rock, sandbagging and sweating under a sun that tried to boil your bones. The men worked like ants on a corpse, never sure if the thing they were building would ever take shape. They knew their part but it was hard to see the whole.

A siren howled through the canyon. Bosses who usually pushed every man to work every minute oddly told their crews --- down tools, head to the edge --- head to the upper coffer dam. Watch. See what you all have helped to build.

They gathered by the hundreds along the ridges, the decks of the catwalks, and the edges of the canyon walls. Hard hats gleamed in the sunlight like coins scattered across the stone. Miles found a perch on a ledge above the upper coffer dam --- a high scaler's view.

Below, the dam held back the swollen brown water like a fist clenched tight. Behind it, somewhere above the canyon walls, men with gloves and wrenches were making history. There was no great lever to pull, no wheel to spin --- but when the time came, the gates on the diversion tunnels would be opened. Tunnels that were 56 feet in diameter and blasted through 3,000 feet of canyon wall. Each one large enough to drive a freight train through. Dug with dynamite and dragged out by hand and machine over almost two years of brutal labor, just to trick the river into obedience.

And then they heard it --- a deep groaning roar like thunder cracking underground. Then came the shudder. The floodgates opened, and the water, no longer restrained, surged forward with primal fury, hungry to find its path. And it did --- smashing into the mouths of the tunnels, exploding in white foam, curling and screaming through the curves of the rock as it disappeared into darkness.

The river turned. Just like that.

Men gasped and hollered as they watched the water behind the dam slowly start to transform from a vast temporary lake, to a sleek flowing river. Some clapped. Some just stared. Miles felt his throat tighten, his breath stuck somewhere between a laugh and a prayer. It was like watching God blink.

And in the hush that followed, a second siren blew. Short, sharp, and familiar. Back to work. The Foreman's voice echoed off the canyon walls. "All crews report tomorrow to the assignment boards. New posts are going up! Get your names checked!"

Just like that, the spell broke. Just like that thousands of dam builders and tunnel diggers would become concrete pourers. Just like that, tomorrow, November 14, 1932, would become just another work day on the dam. New gangs, new work assignments --- carpenters, finishers, crane operators. The river was beaten, but the work had only just begun.

Miles stared for a moment longer. The sound of boots on gravel faded behind him. It was beautiful, he thought --- that the labor wasn't mindless. That the blistered hands and sunburned backs had bent something eternal. That they'd done the impossible.

Still for Miles, it was an empty feeling. No Billy to share it with. It was a feeling less of accomplishment and more of change --- change that wanted to push him somewhere. A feeling that said, 'This is ending for you.'

Chapter 48: A Dime a Dozen

Weeks went by. Still no Billy. Life went on. Sadder, but on. Miles made some mistakes on the ropes that scared him. He wasn't focusing enough. He tried to keep his routine. He tried to enjoy his weekends at Becky's. He tried to be upbeat at dinner with Nancy and Charlie. But he was not succeeding very well. He was annoyed with himself. Life always had to go on. How many times had he pushed

forward? How many times had he forced himself to move on ---
despite anything that happened. Why couldn't he do that with Billy?
He felt life was changing.

Another Saturday night. Another trip into Las Vegas. Another
pleasant visit with Nancy and Charlie. And, of course, some precious
private moments with Becky. But now, as he walked the few blocks
for his usual stay at The Meadows, something gnawed at him --- the
feeling of unfinished business. A feeling of something ending. Billy
was gone. And so was the spark that made work on the dam
tolerable. Without Billy, every shift felt endless, every task heavier.
He constantly wondered where his friend had gone. The rumors
about the high scalers' jobs drying up didn't help either. Change was
coming. But tonight, change had already arrived --- just not in the
way Miles expected.

When he stepped into The Meadows, he immediately noticed the air
was heavier. Not with dust or heat, but something else. Peachy sat
behind the front desk, her usual sharp eyes dulled with worry. She
wasn't counting money, wasn't fussing over a ledger --- just sitting
there, staring at nothing. Miles set his bag down. "Peachy?" She
blinked, as if surprised to see him, then forced a weak smile. "Well,
look who's back. The quiet one." That's what she called Miles before
she really knew him. Most of the other men came in loud and drunk,
sometimes trying to sneak in ladies of the evening. But Miles never
did. She still liked calling him that.

Miles pulled up a chair. "What's wrong?" Peachy sighed, rubbing her
hands over her face before finally answering. "This place is bleeding
me dry, Miles. I can't keep up. The dam workers trash the rooms,
tourists don't want to stay in a dump, the repairs cost too much, and
I can't afford the help to fix it." She exhaled sharply. "The truth is, this
time next week, I might not even be here." Miles frowned. "You're
saying The Meadows is done?" Peachy gave a short laugh, but there
was no humor in it. "I'm saying I am."

Miles sat back, thinking. He wasn't upset for himself --- he could find another place to sleep. But this was Peachy. This was her home. And, if Miles was honest, it had become a part of his home too.

A long silence passed. Then, an idea began to take shape. He leaned forward. "Peachy, I have an idea." She smirked, though her tired eyes, "Ideas are a dime a dozen, kid." Miles grinned, "Good thing you can afford one, then." That got a small chuckle out of her. "Alright, what's this big idea?" Miles shook his head. "Not yet. Just... trust me on this. Give me a week."

Peachy narrowed her eyes. "A week? What's so special about a week?" "That's when I'll tell you. But you gotta promise me you'll still be here." She studied him for a long moment, then sighed. "I guess I can keep this old shack standing for one more week." Miles nodded. "Good." And with that, he headed upstairs, an idea brewing in his mind, something that might just keep The Meadows standing a little longer. And something that might just change his life too. If it worked.

Chapter 49: Camera Lessons

Sundays for Miles and Becky had a rhythm and a routine as predictable as their Saturdays. With Peachy's problems lingering in his mind, they strolled the streets of Las Vegas, always amazed at something new. The city seemed to be growing as rapidly as their relationship always something new and different and exciting. It was a welcome distraction from Billy and Peachy.

Today they strolled Stewart Avenue, amazed at the building progress of the giant Las Vegas Post Office that was almost magically growing as they watched. They admired the smooth, modern lines of the Art Deco architecture, so different from the rougher, hastily built wooden building overwhelmed by the growing city. The scent of fresh concrete surrounded the grand new building. In the distance they saw neon signs flickering to life outside newly opened casinos and restaurants.

Lunch was a picnic in Fremont Park. As usual, Becky was enjoying their precious time together. But Miles was distracted today. His mind seemed to be somewhere else. Miles broke a brief period of silence with a strange question. "Before I get back to the bus, can I borrow a camera and some film from the paper?" Becky answered, "You can borrow a camera, but you won't exactly be borrowing film, will you?" Miles began, "I suppose not, but…" Becky interrupted, looked at him suspiciously, arms crossed. "You're not planning to get yourself into trouble, are you?" "Nothing illegal," he grinned. "Just…a little borrowing. It's a long story, and too soon to tell. I promise I'll bring it back next week." She studied him, trying to figure out what he was up to, but finally sighed. "I'll get it for you."

With only a few precious hours left before his pickup at the bus stop, 4 o'clock sharp, they finished lunch and went to The Desert Sun office. Ramon was there as usual. Becky picked up her mom's spare Graflex Speed Graphic and a big bag of film telling Ramon he'd have the camera back next week. He didn't look happy but he nodded ok.

They went outside. Becky tilted her head. "Miles, you don't even own any photographs, let alone take them. What's this about?" He exhaled. "I just… I need to take some pictures." She realized she wasn't going to get a straight answer, but she trusted him.

"Do you even know how to use this?" Miles forced a sheepish smile. "Not exactly." Becky sighed and sat down beside him. "Alright, listen close. I've watched my mom use these cameras so many times, I think I'm pretty good by now. This camera uses sheet film, not rolls like a Kodak. You load film into these…" She pulled a 4x5-inch film holder from the bag. "Each one holds two shots, one on each side. You have to keep track or you'll double-expose it." She flipped open the camera's back. "First, you slide this in here, behind the ground glass." She demonstrated, locking the film holder in place. "This part is called the dark slide…" She tapped a thin metal sheet on the holder. "You keep this in until you're ready to take the picture. If you pull it too soon, light will ruin the film."

Miles nodded slowly. "Alright... so how do I actually take the picture?" Becky continued. "You focus first." She pointed to the bellows, the accordion-like section between the lens and body. "Turn this knob to move the lens forward and back. Look through here --- " She opened the ground glass viewer at the back. "The image will be upside-down, but once it's sharp, you're in focus."

Miles peered through, squinting. "That's not helpful." "You'll get used to it." She took the camera back and adjusted a small lever near the lens. "Now, this sets your shutter speed --- faster speeds for bright light, slower for dim light. And this..." She pointed to a ring around the lens " --- controls the aperture. That's how much light gets in." Miles scratched his head. "I thought I just press a button." Becky laughed. "Not with this beast. Once you're focused, you pull out the dark slide, then press the shutter release. After that, you put the slide back in so you don't ruin the film." "And then?" "Then you flip the holder over for your second shot, or swap it out for a fresh one." She handed him a small leather pouch. "Don't waste them."

Miles felt the weight of the camera in his hands, suddenly aware of how careful he'd have to be. He still hadn't told her why he needed it, and she didn't ask. Instead, she adjusted the strap over his shoulder. "If you break it," she said lightly, "my mother will have your hide." Miles shrugged. "Then I guess I better not break it."

They practiced as much as they could before the bus arrived. Becky walked Miles to the stop, going over all the steps.

Miles thanked her for her help. "One more thing," he said. "Geez, What now?" Miles answered, "Do you remember where you parked your mom's car that day you came to visit me? Becky blushed and smiled and poked his chest. "By that big boulder? Of course I do," she said slyly. Miles said seriously, not much time before the bus came, "It's not like that Becky. Listen carefully please. I need you and Charlie to meet me there Friday night, eight o'clock sharp. Have Charlie drive his Ice House truck. I'm sure you can get a favor from him" "What?" Becky was confused. Miles said, "I don't have time to explain. Do you trust me?" "With my life." Then, please do it, it's important. I love you." Realizing they had never said that to each other yet, Becky glowed, "I love you too."

Camera in one hand film in the other, Miles kissed Becky softly goodbye.

Chapter 50: Mission Part One

Monday morning, as usual, Miles trudged onto the work truck with the other high scalers. But today, he had something else with him besides his lunch bucket. He found a seat near the back of the truck. Tucked neatly to one side, he concealed Nancy's camera and film. Today would not be a regular work day. He hoped it wouldn't be his last. He had something else to do. Something more important. Something dangerous. A mission. A mission supervisors would not approve of. A mission he wanted to keep secret. A mission that would take all week. A mission that would have to be done in four carefully planned parts.

He'd have to do the hardest part of his mission right away. Without it, the rest didn't matter. He moved quickly, discretely carrying Nancy's camera and the film cannisters. He'd be the first man on the ropes today, as usual, to avoid any suspicion. But today, instead of taking center stage as usual, Miles picked a distant location on the far end of the day's work line. He set Nancy's camera on the ground and stuffed the film cannisters inside his pants pockets, sliding some that wouldn't fit under his belt. Certain no one would see, he tossed his tools on the ground, making empty slots in his tool belt. He took a deep breath and wiped sweat off of his face.

He was as ready as he'd ever be to swing out on the ropes and take the pictures he needed. He wasn't afraid of being seen by his co-workers. If the other scalers were doing their work properly, they'd be watching their own work. He was far more afraid of dropping the camera and losing what would likely be his only opportunity for taking these pictures --- and of course, he refused to think about what he was most afraid of --- using both hands to take pictures with a camera 800 feet above the bottom of the canyon.

Wind pounded his face. The last thing he needed today was a windy day. Pulse pounding in his head, he positioned himself on the edge of a scaffolding, He took a couple of practice shots: the workers below, the massive cranes swinging into action, a muck cart rolling out of Arizona Tunnel Two, a few shots of the coffer dams, a shot of the dry river basin below with its water held captive upstream. But these stunning images would not be enough. He needed pictures from out on the ropes.

Gripping the camera tightly, Miles swung himself out over the edge of the scaffolding, dangling from the ropes. The wind howled around him, but he ignored it, focusing entirely on the camera. The only sound he could hear was the faint click of the camera's shutter as he quickly framed the shot. He snapped a photo of the worksite, then another of the crew, then another of the canyon walls rising up beneath him. He stored used cannisters in his empty toolbelt and took fresh ones from his pockets to re-load, never looking down.

Miles swung lower, catching the movement of the workers below as they climbed the scaffolding, the ropes creaking under their weight. Then he pointed the camera across the open air directly at another high scaler in action. The photo would be perfect --- raw, real, full of motion. This was the photo that would show just how dangerous this work was, how every moment was a tightrope walk between life and death.

Each shot felt like a dare. Each click of the shutter was a promise to himself that he would get it right, that he wouldn't let this chance slip away. He took photos of the ropes, the tools, the sky above, the men below. He wanted everything. The mundane and the extraordinary. The everyday and the life-threatening.

When the last shot was taken, he slowly pulled himself back onto solid ground, his body aching from the strain but his mind alive with the thrill of what he had just done. The camera hung heavy around his neck, but he didn't feel its weight now. He felt the rush of being alive after a death-defying risk.

He'd lost several hours of work today taking the photos. Lost work that would surely be noticed. But he could see the pictures in his head. He knew it was worth it. Tomorrow the camera would have one more day of work. Then he could move on to the other parts of his mission.

Chapter 51: Mission Part Two

The next day, Miles knew what was coming. Jackie Bee, his foreman, didn't even wait until Miles went to the truck. He met Miles in the barracks and got right in Miles's face intentionally in front of the other men, "Tornero, your work site looked like shit yesterday. What the hell go into you boy? Pull another stunt like that and you're outta here. I don't give a damn if you're the best. Now move it!"

Miles convincingly hung his head as if shamed. The words stung. He knew the foreman was right. But yesterday had to be done. Jackie moved on to other business. Miles slinked back to his bunk, reached under, grabbed Nancy's camera and some fresh film and left the used cannisters for development hidden under the bed. He was ready for part two of his mission.

He knew he'd have to perform today. So, he kept his plan for today simple. Work the ropes, do a great job, take just a little time to take some photos from solid ground. Relief coursed through his body as he realized he didn't have to wrestle with that camera from the ropes. The only tricky part for today was concealing the noise of the camera --- certainly not designed for secrecy. Luckily every day on a high scaler's work site was filled with powerful noises. Compressors, jackhammers, cranes, rock drills, and dynamite blasts that he hoped would drown it out.

Miles worked with extra focus and speed that day. He could not afford to stay on Jackie Bee's bad side if he wanted to complete his mission. During lunch and in between swings over the edge to smooth the canyon's rough surfaces, he snapped pictures of the workers as they climbed, hammered, and chiseled away at the massive stone. He took pictures of the truck that brought them all to the site --- the beast that also transported the tools and the material that fueled the dam's construction. He took photos of everything from men guzzling water and sleeping in the shade to men swinging sledgehammers and setting dynamite fuses. The air was thick with dust; he hoped some of the images would reflect a grainy reality.

Miles tucked the camera out of site and finished his work day --- double time and double perfect. Jackie Bee strolled by, "Back to normal boy, don't backslide." After the truck brought the men back to the barracks, Miles trudged to his bunk stashed the camera and film and hoped he'd never have to take another photo in his life.

Chapter 52: Mission Part Three

Monday and Tuesday with the camera were a success. Part three would be tricky but doable, but no camera. It might be a little time consuming. He might ruffle Jackie Bee's feathers again. But he had to take the risk.

This morning when he boarded the truck, he had something else to conceal---a large, but tightly folded, duffle bag that he purchased at the company store using some of his last remaining scrip. Last night, as the others slept, Miles carefully painted a warning on the outside of the duffle, 'Do Not Touch: Property of J.R. Mellinger." Mellinger was likely the meanest regional foreman any of the men could think of. He'd come around every week or two and if everything wasn't in tip top shape, heads would roll. No one seemed to pay attention to Miles's extra baggage today, and he was glad for that.

When the truck came to a stop and the men poured out, Miles did not lead the pack. He was not the first out on the ropes as usual. He hoped Jackie Bee didn't notice. Instead, he quietly wandered away to the high scaler's trash heap. While Six Companies seemed to cut corners just about everywhere, they never seemed to do so with high scaler equipment. Every rope and every harness needed to be fresh and strong. Every pickaxe had to be sturdy and secure. When pitons were bent, they were instantly discarded. The slightest wobble in a bosun chair made it obsolete. Damaged sledgehammers were replaced with brand new ones --- same with crowbars, worn gloves and dented helmets.

Miles looked at the impressive pile with amazement and anger. Amazed at how readily Six Companies was willing to throw away so much equipment. Angry because he knew the reason had much less to do with safety, and much more to do with the difficulty the employer had replacing any high scaler killed or injured. Using only ideal equipment helped.

He'd have to accomplish his mission today in stages. If all went well, he'd do the same thing Thursday and Friday. Miles quickly hid the empty duffle beside the trash heap. He planned that each time he finished a session on the ropes he'd make a quick trip to the trash heap, add a few things to the duffle, and get right back to work. He was confident he could hurry through his work assignments fast enough to keep Jackie Bee unaware. He knew how dangerous it was to rush on the ropes, but he'd taken many chances before, and this one was worth it.

He'd have no choice to be fast --- someone was always watching if you didn't go to the ropes on time. "Hey Tornero!" a co-worker yelled at Miles, "You plan on doin' any work today?" Tugging at his zipper, Miles shouted from the trash heap, "Jesus, can't a fella take a leak in private around here."

Miles knew he had to get to the ropes right away to avoid suspicion. But there would be time today to gradually fill the duffle. Each time Miles visited the trash heap, he'd find the best pieces he could --- lengths of rope, pickaxes, pitons, gloves, dust-covered helmets, anything that smelled of hard work and danger. He knew the penalty for stealing from the work site was instant dismissal and possible legal action. But he wasn't stealing. This was trash.

At the end of the day, Miles made sure he was first to the truck. He grabbed the duffle full of worksite trash and hoisted it into the truck, making sure the sign he painted was clearly visible. If anyone was curious about the contents of that bag, they'd have to be pretty brave to mess with it --- or else face the wrath of J.R. Mellinger.

When the truck pulled up, Miles was sure to be last out. He lingered a few moments until everyone cleared. He slid the duffle off the back of the truck, hoisted it on his shoulder, and carried the bag to the big boulder where Becky parked her car the day she visited Miles. He emptied the duffle behind the boulder, went back to the barracks and stashed the bag under his bed. Then he walked to the mess hall for dinner.

Chapter 53: By the Big Boulder

Miles repeated his trash collection routine on Thursday and Friday. Three days of deliveries of a duffle filled to capacity made the pile of old tools almost as big as the boulder.

Now --- on Friday evening, he waited for Charlie and Becky. He thought 8 o'clock would never come. He circled the barracks, he paced the hallways, he sat on a stoop and threw pebbles at a hole. One more hour --- and he prayed to God that Charlie and Becky would be at the boulder.

At 7:45, Miles went back to the barracks and quietly crouched on the floor. He reached under his bunk, dragging out Nancy's camera and the film to be developed. Then he stepped out into the night.

Miles arrived at the boulder just as Charlie's headlights appeared in the distance. The truck rumbled to a stop. Charlie looked out the driver's seat window at Miles and laughed, "Your girlfriend can be very convincing!" Mile smiled back, "I thought she would be." Becky came running around the truck and hugged Miles. "Thank you," he said. They kissed. The two men shook hands. Charlie asked, "What in the world is going on?"

Miles didn't answer at first. Instead, he handed Becky the camera. "Here's your mom's camera, and here's a whole bunch of film. I need you to develop it, and have it all ready by Saturday. Make it look really nice. Frames, matts, whatever it takes. Bring them all to The Meadows on Saturday night after the bus arrives --- about seven o'clock, right when I get to The Meadows. Can you do that?" Becky stumbled, "Um, maybe, yes. Yes, I can but..." Miles interrupted, "Please, I'll explain Saturday."

Miles led Charlie and Becky behind the boulder. "Help me get this stuff on the truck. I'll explain everything Saturday when I get into town, okay?" "Um, I guess," said Charlie. As they loaded the last tools onto the truck, miles shot them another wave of confusion. "I need you to bring this to Peachy's hotel. Pile it all in her lobby. Tell her I'll explain it all Saturday." Charlie gave up trying to make sense of what Miles was doing. He opened the truck door, and patted Miles on the shoulder, "You sure have a lot of explaining to do. We'll see you Saturday."

Chapter 54: More than one Proposal

When Saturday finally came, Miles could barely sit still on the Saturday Night Special. He hoped Becky had the photos ready. He hoped Charlie had delivered the tools.

By the time he reached The Meadows, Peachy was waiting for him at the front desk, half-smiling, half-skeptical. "Well? You got your grand idea ready? And what's the big idea having Charlie put all this junk in the middle of my damn lobby!" Before Miles could answer, Becky walked in, right on time, a big box in her hands. Charlie strolled behind, joined by Nancy. "Wow," Miles said, "Everybody's here. Perfect."

Miles turned to Peachy, "Peachy, you and I are going to be partners." Give me five minutes to make my pitch. Then decide if you're in, okay? "Partners?" Peachy asked. "Are you goin' crazy, boy? Ain't nobody wants to partner with me in this dump." Miles asked again,

"Just hear me out, okay?" Peachy said, "What have I got to lose? Nuthin.' Go ahead."

Miles went over to the pile and began handling the artifacts --- ropes coiled like sleeping snakes, rusted pickaxes, a dented old helmet. He laid some out methodically on a counter, like cards in a winning hand, each to tell a story, each a part of his vision.

Peachy picked up a rope and squinted at it. "Are we opening up a damn museum?" She scoffed, "What am I looking at here?" "History," Miles said. "People come from all over the world and come to Las Vegas to see progress on the dam. They're fascinated by it. We're gonna make this hotel a part of that story. A place where they can sleep inside the legend. Peachy, I propose we say goodbye to The Meadows and rename this place the High Scaler!"

Miles hoped the photos would seal the deal. He tossed aside the tools that he would use to decorate his new idea. Then he took the box from Becky, appreciation in his eyes for her developing them all so quickly. He opened the box and looked at the photos. Some were framed, some enlarged, some stapled to simple carboard placards. Miles had not yet seen them, but as he unpacked them, he felt the chill of their splendor.

Each image revealed the raw essence of life atop Black Canyon. One showed high scalers suspended in mid-air --- their silhouettes etched against the vast expanse. Another showed the rugged terrain: jagged rocks bathed in relentless sunlight, a testament to the harsh environment these men braved daily. He loved most the shots of men swinging above the canyon. Candid shots captured workers guzzling water, their faces etched with exhaustion, another of a worker sleeping while dripping with sweat. Close-ups of the equipment ---- weathered ropes, heavy drills, and shimmering helmets --- conveyed the rawness of their tools and the ingenuity required to operate in such a formidable setting. Collectively, these photographs brought to life the experience of working 800 feet above the canyon floor.

Miles saw Peachy's eyes widen, a good sign. Charlie rubbed his chin. Nancy smiled with interest. Becky beamed with pride. Miles went on, "This hotel will sing with the history of the men who built this dam. Every item on that counter and in that pile is an original artifact." Peachy took a deep breath. Her skeptical frown quickly began to melt.

"You really think people would pay to stay in a place like this?" she asked. Miles leaned against the counter, grinning. "I think they'll be lining up." Peachy let out a long, slow sigh. "Well, hell, partner, I guess we'd better start fixing up the place."

The group erupted in cheers, their collective joy filling the space. They gathered around the counter and began touching and handling the artifacts and holding the photos, making the idea of the High Scaler Hotel spring to life. As they examined the items, ideas flowed freely. Charlie suggested, "That sledgehammer would make a great centerpiece above the bar." Nancy held her favorite photo, "This one captures their spirit; it belongs in the lobby, to greet every guest." Becky, caressed a thick worn rope, "This could be woven into the decor, right there in the lounge."

Ideas flowed. Hearts raced. Action was in the air. Miles felt happy but somehow --- incomplete. He watched Becky with admiration as she raced up a staircase to show where she thought a photo should go. He thought back to how she added his name to the hire list, how she trusted him with Max's poison, how she trusted him when he knocked on the door of the employment office to meet her for the first time, how she took a chance with her mom's car to come visit him, how she trusted him with her mom's camera, how she never wavered when he asked her to come back to Boulder City with Charlie even though she had no idea why. In that moment, he realized why he felt incomplete.

"Becky," he called. She turned and answered from the staircase. "What?" Miles swallowed hard. "Come down here for a second."

Becky rolled her eyes but climbed down, taking careful care with the photo as she walked.

Miles took her hand. She looked at him, confused. "Miles?" He looked at her with a look she'd not yet seen in him. Nancy, Charlie, and Peachy looked confused. "Most everything I've ever done in my life I've had to do alone. I don't want to do that anymore." He dropped to one knee. Becky gasped. The photo fell to the ground. "Rebecca McGuire," Miles said, looking up at her, grinning like a fool, "We're going to build this place together, side by side. Now I want to build something else with you --- a life. Marry me."

Becky's hands flew to her face. For the first time in her life, she was speechless. Then, in a flash, she threw herself at him, nearly knocking him over. "Yes! Of course, yes!"

Nancy cried. Charlie grinned and clapped Miles on the back. "Well, you got yourself a hell of a woman there, son." Then Charlie paused. He looked at Nancy. Looked back at Miles and Becky. Then suddenly, like he'd just made up his mind, he dropped to one knee. "Hell, if these two kids are getting hitched, why shouldn't we?" Nancy, we've been dancing around this for too long. Let's just do it already." Nancy laughed, "How can I say no to a man who took me all the way to Los Angeles and back?" She shouted, "Yes!"

Chapter 55: Las Vegas Style

It was a simple double wedding, Las Vegas style --- quick, joyful, and surrounded by the people who mattered most. No grand ballrooms, no lavish orchestras, no drawn-out ceremonies. Just two couples, side by side, exchanging vows with nothing but love and promise ahead of them.

Miles and Becky. Charlie and Nancy. It had been Charlie's idea to marry together, laughing as he said, "Why the hell not? If we're all in, let's go all in." And so they did.

They could take advantage of getting married in Nevada --- no waiting, no blood tests, and the Clark County Courthouse, always a busy place for couples looking to tie the knot, was open 24 hours a day. They chose one of the small but respectable chapels in town, the kind that had seen all sorts of couples over the years --- young lovers running off in a hurry, out-of-towners looking for a thrill, and folks like them, standing steady with full hearts, ready to step into the next chapter of their lives.

Peachy was there, of course, grinning ear to ear, beaming with pride for Miles. Andy, Charlie's right-hand man at the Ice House, stood tall, clearly honored to witness the moment. Ramon, ever the observer, made mental notes for the next edition of The Desert Sun, but made sure he took a break from work to celebrate.

Happiness filled the chapel. Laughter, toasts, promises whispered between lovers. The weight of the past --- the struggles, the losses --- felt lighter today, like they had finally made it through the hardest part.

And yet, as Miles stood with Becky's hand in his, a deep pang of sorrow settled in his chest. Billy. He should have been here. Miles could almost see him --- grinning, maybe cracking a joke about Miles finally settling down, his hat pushed back like it always was. But Billy was gone, lost to the very work that had brought them all here.

Becky squeezed his hand, as if she knew what he was thinking. Maybe she did. He took a breath, pushed through the ache, and looked ahead. There was so much to look forward to—their life together, their home, rebuilding The Meadows and turning it into something even greater than before.

As the ceremony ended, the couples turned to face their friends, their new life stretching out before them. There would be celebrations tonight, laughter, and the promise of the future --- but tomorrow, they would return to the work that had brought them all together. The Meadows wouldn't rebuild itself, and neither would the future they had envisioned.

Chapter 56: The Road to the Vision

Miles had never felt such relief in his life. He had no idea what Peachy might say, but he had had to try. Now, he was done with the dam. No more waking up in a sweltering bunkhouse before dawn. No more hanging by a rope over certain death while the foremen barked orders like drill sergeants. No more looking over his shoulder, wondering if someone else would mysteriously disappear the way Billy had. He didn't even bother telling them he quit. After what they did to Billy, they didn't deserve it.

Miles threw himself headfirst into his new mission --- turning The Meadows Hotel into The High Scaler Hotel and building something of his own. He and Becky moved into one of the shabby rooms at The Meadows, determined to fix every peeling wall, every creaky floorboard, every leaky pipe. Each refurbished room would have a canyon theme with at least one photo and one authentic artifact. More than that, the lobby would become a living breathing testament to all the workers who put their back breaking labor into the dam, especially the high scalers. The run-down hotel became his new worksite.

Becky resigned from the employment office. She belonged here now. She was a steady force that kept Miles's creative mind grounded, the perfect complement to his raw energy. They worked together seamlessly, bouncing ideas off each other, her keen eye for detail making her invaluable. She never knew --- how would she know in the world she came from --- that she had a remarkable flair for color, balance, symmetry, design offering suggestions on textures, and tones that would transform the hotel into something extraordinary.

Miles learned that Peachy didn't just sit at a desk. She could keep track of dozens of things going on. She wrote everything down, made a strict budget, controlled expenses, kept schedules, tracked orders. It wasn't long before everyone knew Peachy made all the trains run on time.

Miles was grateful to even have a budget. And he owed it all to Charlie. After grueling work at the Ice House all day, Charlie wasn't too interested in helping out with physical labor. He did help occasionally, especially with carpentry skills that came in handy from time to time --- but he had something far more important to offer --- connections. Charlie was a respected business owner. He pulled a few strings. In two days from the day Peachy agreed to partner, Miles and Peachy had a bank loan ---hopefully enough to make things work. And to top it all off, Charlie was happy to offer the services of his truck.

Nancy and Ramon were busy at The Desert Sun. It wasn't easy for them to roll up their sleeves and pitch in either. But they too had other things to offer. Nancy would give them free advertising space in the paper when they needed it and meanwhile Ramon was sure to keep subtle hints cooking in each edition of the paper, offering clear hints that something special was going on at the old Meadows hotel, closed now for renovations. Nancy had long given up on having to make hiring decisions at the paper. Ever since Ramon started hiring, everyone who walked in the door was a great worker --- friends and family of Ramon cut from the same cloth. Ramon had plenty more, so, Miles had plenty of quality labor. Ramon's daughter Petra was a gifted artist, never taken seriously or well-accepted in a prejudiced Las Vegas. She began painting beautiful murals on the walls of the lobby --- she didn't ask much in pay from Peachy and Miles, she was hoping for recognition.

Everyone had a role to play. Miles was the director. As they moved from one project to the next, each piece of the lobby slowly came to life. At one time everyone had talked about having Petra paint boulders and rocky cliffs on the walls. But Charlie said, "She can paint a lot of beautiful things, but why don't we just bring in real boulders?" With the help of Charlie's truck and Ramon's laborers the lobby had dozens of boulders of various sizes adding depth and grit to whatever it might become.

But there was one particular boulder shrouded in mystery. It stood inexplicably in the center of the lobby. It was out of place --- its size, its form, even its texture, stood in stark contrast to the other boulders. Petra had asked to go on the truck when they gathered the boulders. She had seen this boulder and insisted they bring it back --- so large it required a separate trip. No one really knew what it would become, but it was as if the Boulder itself was an integral part of something far bigger than anyone could yet understand. Except perhaps for Petra.

There was a strange mix of chaos and organization to the work. The rooms and the lobby were far from finished, but even in the chaos, there was a strange sense of purpose. Ropes, hammers, spikes, and unmarked crates filled the space --- each piece a mystery, each seemingly allowed to select its place, everything at once unclear but essential. Every corner seemed to hide something new, something unfinished, yet unmistakably important.

Miles stood in the center of it all, rubbing his eyes from lack of sleep, but he was far too absorbed to let fatigue slow him. There was a vision in his mind, a vision he saw so clearly that sometimes, he thought it was already finished. But it wasn't. Not yet.

Peachy asked Miles if they could make one lobby wall look like the wall of the canyon. They had enough rope to hang several all the way down from the ceiling, and enough boulders to pile all along the wall, the rest of the wall a simulation of a canyon cliff. Peachy wasn't much for ideas, but this one kept popping into her head. "We'll let the guests pretend to hang from the ropes and let them dress up like high scalers and put a camera there and have their picture taken --- then we'll sell it to 'em," She laughed --- but Miles thought it was a great idea.

Petra asked Miles to consider another idea. Something that would make everything come together, A massive mural of some kind. She needed him to trust her. She could not define it --- only feel it. Her energy was so sharp, so convincing, he had to say yes.

The photographs were Mile's most important part. But how they would work was still unclear. Some were framed and already beginning to find their place on the walls, some seemed lost. They were scattered across the room --- on tables, tucked in corners --- and yet their meanings were hidden, their stories still incomplete.

The building was alive with tension, with anticipation. Every corner held a secret. Every step of the process was clouded in mystery, like the final pieces of a complex puzzle being slowly slid into place.

Chapter 57: I think We're Done

Somehow it all came together. On no particular day at no particular time, Miles, Becky, Peachy, Charlie, Nancy, Petra, and the rest of the crew found themselves in the middle of the lobby --- paralyzed by their surroundings. Miles whispered, "I think we're done."

Petra's mural surrounded them on all sides. A powerful Nevada sun, painted on the ceiling, glared from above. The walls looked like canyon walls holding scaffolding and busy men. The floor gave the illusion of walking above the empty river bed, a maze of complex imaginary work going on.

Peachy's rock wall and camera station stood ready for business. The bar, the lounge, and front desk were all themed work stations with tools and artifacts skillfully placed and coordinated under Becky's watchful eye. Miles was finally happy where every photo was placed --- telling the story just the way he imagined.

Everything in the lobby coalesced in a panorama of life working high above Black Canyon. But the most stunning of all was the giant boulder that sat in the middle of the lobby. It was now a sculpture, carved by Petra --- using only the same jackhammers and chisels the men used to conquer the canyon walls. It was crude and rugged, but captivating. From any angle a viewer could see what looked like the faces of men --- dozens, scores maybe ---emerging from deep within the rock. Was this one wearing a hat? Was that one smiling? Was this one suffering? The answer always seemed to depend on who you asked.

The sculpture demanded viewers to see what they saw, not what the artist saw. It seemed to shout in raw primitive terms about man's relationship with nature. When Miles first saw Petra's completed work, he gasped, taken back years ago to the day he watched the barges working on the Bayonne Bridge with Max. His words echoed in Miles's head, "Man don't seem to stand up too well against nature, Butchie, but sometimes all it takes is time. Mother Nature always wins when she wants to win, but if man is strong enough, if he tries his best, she can be a good mother. Sometimes, given time, she lets man feel like he can make a difference."

Chapter 58: Open For Business

The High Scaler Hotel quickly became a Las Vegas sensation. Miles intentionally bypassed a grand opening, steering clear of formalities and city officials. He envisioned the hotel as a tribute to the high scalers --- the unsung heroes of the dam's construction --- not as a corporate venture.

Guests were lucky to get a room. Those unable to secure a reservation came just to visit, often spending time at the bar or capturing memories at Peachy's booth. The lobby was constantly busy. Miles loved his role as the unofficial host, sharing tales from his high scaling days and offering insights into the triumphs and struggles of the dam workers. Guests enjoyed the authenticity of engaging with a genuine high scaler.

The years were kind to the High Scaler Hotel. Miles often reflected on the risks he'd taken, grateful for the rewards --- not just in financial success but for the sense of purpose.

Chapter 59: The End of an Era

Miles strolled through the front door of The Desert Sun, a sturdy box tucked in one arm. The office was alive with the clatter of newsroom noise as Ramon pieced together the next edition. He spotted Nancy at her usual post --- her desk overflowing with notes, ink-stained fingers flipping through the latest wire reports. He set the box down with a thud. "Brought those supplies you asked for." Nancy barely looked up, "About time. Put 'em next to the cabinet."

Miles had a full day ahead at the hotel, but he wasn't in any hurry to rush out just yet. The Desert Sun had always fascinated him --- the way a single room filled with ink and paper could keep a whole town informed. He was particularly fascinated by how a small-town newspaper could get news from across the nation. He watched as Ramon swiftly scanned the perforated tapes, filled with coded information from faraway places that would soon be converted to readable print. He grabbed a cup of coffee from the percolator in the corner and lingered near Ramon's desk, scanning the latest front-page article as the editor rolled it out. One article immediately caught his eye.

BOULDER DAM NEARS COMPLETION

Miles took a slow sip, letting the words settle. It was official. The last bucket of concrete had been poured, the final calculations checked --- and rechecked. The dam construction was done.

But there was still work left to do.

The article laid it out in crisp, no-nonsense sentences; the construction camp, once teeming with thousands of workers, was slowly being dismantled. The company store, once a lifeline for supplies, was being deconstructed. Temporary office shacks, makeshift dormitories, and tool yards were being cleared away. The rail lines that had delivered steel and cement were being dismantled, their purpose fulfilled. The massive overhead cableways, once swinging hundreds of feet above the canyon with concrete-filled buckets, were being taken down piece by piece. Even the huge cooling pipes, used to keep the concrete from curing too fast, were being removed.

And yet, in the middle of all this deconstruction, one thing would remain: Boulder City.

Miles lifted an eyebrow as he read on. The government had made an unexpected decision: rather than tearing down the town as originally planned, they would keep it. Boulder City had proven itself to be more than just a temporary camp --- it was a functioning, orderly community, far removed from the lawlessness of Las Vegas. The federal government saw value in maintaining it as a permanent settlement, a hub for dam operations and the people who would manage the great structure in the years to come.

Miles smirked at the irony. In the beginning, Boulder City had been built to be erased, but now it would outlive the project itself.

"Seems like a damn shame to be wiping away so much of what we built," Ramon muttered, leaning back in his chair. "But I suppose it has to be done."

Miles nodded. "Yeah. Funny thing, though --- Boulder City stays." Ramon snorted. "I guess the government likes having a town it can control." Miles didn't argue. He sipped his coffee, eyes drifting back to the article. The final lines confirmed what he had already heard in town: President Franklin D. Roosevelt was coming for the dedication ceremony. September 30, 1935. His gaze lingered on the words. It was history in the making, the culmination of years of struggle, sweat, and sacrifice. He thought back to his first days on the project --- arriving as just another hungry laborer, surviving the brutal heat, dodging death on the cliffs. And now here he was, a successful hotel owner, reading about the near completion of the dam that had changed his life. Then, something else caught his eye.

BOULDER DAM DEDICATION BY FDR SET FOR SEPTEMBER 30

He exhaled slowly. Boulder Dam. Not Hoover Dam.

In his younger days Miles never had time to understand political debates, so the dam's name struck him as particularly convoluted.

Best he could tell, it seemed that every time someone new became President, the dam's name changed. At first, it was called "Boulder Dam." That made some sense to him because at some point they wanted to build the dam in Boulder Canyon --- but they changed the location and built it in Black Canyon. But they apparently didn't want to bother changing the name. But then, when Herbert Hoover was president, the name switched to "Hoover Dam." Then, when Roosevelt defeated Hoover, they changed it back to Boulder Dam.

He'd heard somewhere that without Hoover, the dam's planning would never have launched. People said he wrangled states into agreement, pushed for funding, made it possible --- so the dam deserved his name. But Miles also thought back to his own journey --- the hungry days spent in a "Hooverville," scrounging for work, parting ways with Billy in the chaos of it all. Back then, Hoover's name had been spoken in bitterness, a reminder of broken promises and suffering. And yet, here was the most ambitious engineering feat of the age, competing to bear his name.

Whatever this dam was called, he had to be at that dedication. He had to stand there, in front of the dam, and see the finished structure. He knew it wouldn't be turned on yet --- something to do with "hydroelectric" work. But --- all the concrete was poured, all the tunnels drilled. He had to see it.

Draining his coffee cup, Miles set it down and dusted off his hands. He turned toward the door, nodding once to Nancy as he passed. "See you later," he said. She waved him off without looking up. "Say hi to Becky." "Will do." With that, he stepped out into the bright Nevada sun, his mind already on September 30. One last moment with the dam.

Chapter 60: September 30, 1935

Miles stood before the mirror, tying his tie with slow precision. The silk felt smooth beneath his fingers, finer than anything he ever folded as a boy at Charles Grotsky's Fine Men's wear, seemingly now another lifetime ago in Bayonne. He thought back to the day at the shop when he said to himself, "One day I'll wear a suit like that, I know it." He adjusted the knot, straightened his lapels, and turned.

Becky sat on the edge of the bed, watching him, a soft smile on her lips. "Handsome," she said, pushing herself up. The movement was different now. Slower. Heavier. Her dress, beautiful as it was, did little to hide the roundness of her belly. Miles looked at her --- not just at her form, but at what she carried. Their future.

"You ready?" he asked, holding out his hand. Becky nodded. "Are you?" Miles thought for a moment. Ready? For the dam? For returning to a place he hadn't been to in two years? For the memories? For the weight of it all? "I suppose," he said. They walked out together.

They sat on a park bench viewing the dam from a distance. The crowd was everywhere. Men in their Sunday best. Women in their finest dresses. Journalists. Engineers. Workers who once poured the now hardened concrete. And in the center of it all, President Roosevelt. He spoke of industry, of progress, of how the dam transformed the West --- how it transformed America itself. "This is an engineering victory of the first order --- another great achievement of American resourcefulness, skill, and determination. We have turned a raging, untamed river into a source of power and prosperity. This dam stands not only as a triumph of science and labor but as a testament to the vision of those who dared to dream of harnessing the Colorado."

The crowd cheered. But Miles barely heard any of it. His eyes were on the dam. Gaze fixed, he was looking at both his past and his future --- most of his greatest victories, and deepest wounds. He saw himself, hanging from a rope, feet scraping against rock. He saw Billy, grinning through dust-caked skin. He saw blood soaking through boots and men swallowing their grief. He saw the day he left and his refusal to return. He saw something he helped build --- and something that helped build him.

The dam stood as it always would, unmoving, unshakable. Miles exhaled. His hand drifted to his side, grazing Becky's. She took it, her fingers threading through his. She was warm. Real. Alive. He looked at her belly again, then back to the dam. There was talk in the news of war on the horizon. Of a man named Hitler. Of something called "rearmament" in Europe. The world was shifting. But for today --- for this moment --- Miles let himself rest. He had built something. A life. A family. A future. And for the first time in years, he finally knew who he was. The future --- whatever it held --- could wait until tomorrow.

"You're crying," Becky whispered. Miles hadn't realized. He wiped at his cheek, then let out a small, breathy laugh, "Guess I am." Becky said nothing. She squeezed his hand, giving him the space to feel whatever he needed to feel.

The sun broke through the clouds. The light glinted off the great, impossible structure. Miles looked up at it, then higher into the sky, his throat tight, his heart full. He absent-mindedly tapped his belt. His left leg began bouncing --- rapid and powerful. He quieted his leg, and without thinking, without meaning to, he whispered, "thank you, Max."

The End

f18452ac-06ed-4ab7-ba18-a4f1f7a39dc9R01